Moby-Dick Reversed: A Whale's Humorous Account

Classics Reimagined: A Comedic Twist, Volume 2

Said Al Azri

Published by Said Al Azri, 2024.

This is a work of fiction. Similarities to real people, places, or events are entirely coincidental.

MOBY-DICK REVERSED: A WHALE'S HUMOROUS ACCOUNT

First edition. January 27, 2024.

Copyright © 2024 Said Al Azri.

ISBN: 979-8223913962

Written by Said Al Azri.

Also by Said Al Azri

Classics Reimagined: A Comedic Twist
Echoes of Venice: A Modern Tale of Redemption
Moby-Dick Reversed: A Whale's Humorous Account
Treasure Island: The Parrot's Perspective

Family and Parenting Dynamics
From My Heart to Yours: Messages of Love and Learning for My
Child
Balancing Family Life: Strategies for Modern Parenting

Heartstrings: Tales of Valentine's Verse
Verses of the Heart: A Poetic Journey Through Love's Whimsy
Verses of the Heart 2: A Poetic Journey Through Love's Whimsy

Living Fully After 50 Series
Rediscovering Hobbies and Passions After 50
Rediscovering Hobbies and Passions After 50, Book 2
Happiness in the Second Half: Finding Joy and Fulfillment After 50

Table of Contents

To Maida, my guiding star in the vast ocean of life, and **our wonderful children,** who fill our world with joy and laughter.

May this tale bring as many smiles to your faces as you have brought to my heart.

With all my love, Said

Main Characters and Venues

Main Characters:

Moby, the Narrator Whale:

Our main character and narrator, Moby, is not your typical whale. He's articulate, witty, and has a penchant for sarcasm. With a degree in Whale Philosophy (from the University of the Atlantic, no less), Moby offers a humorous and insightful perspective on the events unfolding around him. His commentary on human behavior and ocean life is as enlightening as it is entertaining.

Captain Ahab:

Reimagined as a tech-savvy but still obsession-driven captain, Ahab is the CEO of Pequod Inc., a modern whaling company. He's equipped with the latest in maritime technology, which he uses in his relentless pursuit of Moby. Despite his high-tech arsenal, Ahab is humorously outwitted at every turn by our clever narrator.

The Crew of the Pequod:

A diverse group of sailors who could easily double as a tech support team. They are a mix of seasoned sea veterans and young tech enthusiasts, all caught up in Ahab's obsession. Their interactions and attempts to keep up with Ahab's demands add a comical layer to the story.

Starbuck, the First Mate:

A voice of reason amidst the madness, Starbuck is the Pequod's tech-savvy first mate, who secretly loves marine biology. He often finds himself torn between following Ahab's wild plans and his own rational instincts.

Queequeg, the Harpooner:

Now a drone operator rather than a traditional harpooner, Queequeg is an expert in drone technology but has a soft spot for sea creatures, often missing his target on purpose.

Ishmael, the Storyteller:

A blogger who joins the Pequod to write about his adventures at sea. His humorous blog posts provide a secondary narrative thread that complements Moby's storytelling.

Main Venues:

The Pequod 2.0:

No longer just a whaling ship, the Pequod is now a high-tech vessel, complete with a drone fleet, advanced tracking systems, and a state-of-the-art command center. It's like Silicon Valley met the high seas.

The Ocean:

Presented as a character in its own right, the ocean is a vast, dynamic backdrop to Moby's tale. It's a world of underwater canyons, vibrant coral reefs, and bustling marine life, all described with a touch of humor and wonder.

Nantucket Port:

The modernized port is a bustling hub of activity, where traditional sea lore blends with contemporary culture. It's a place where one can overhear sailors debating the latest in maritime technology over a cup of artisanal seaweed tea.

The Underwater World:

A colorful and lively depiction of the ocean's depths, where Moby introduces us to a variety of quirky sea creatures, each with their own humorous traits and stories.

In "Moby-Dick Reversed: A Whale's Humorous Account," the legendary tale is retold with a unique blend of humor and modernity. Each character is carefully crafted to add depth and amusement to the story, while the venues are vividly described, transforming the classic setting into a lively and engaging world that resonates with contemporary readers.

Act 1: The Whale's Introduction

<=><=>*<=>*<=>*<=>*<=>*

Scene 1: The Whale's Monologue

<=><=>*<=>*<=>*<=>*<=>*

In the vast, undulating expanse of the ocean, where the blue seems infinite and the depths unfathomable, I reside. My name? Well, in the annals of human literature, I am known as Moby Dick, the great white whale, the leviathan, the ocean's most elusive celebrity. But between us, let's keep it simple – just call me Moby.

Ah, let me take you back to where it all started, at the bustling Nantucket Port. You should have seen it! Old-world charm tangling with the new age like seaweed in the surf. Sailors there were humming traditional sea shanties while babbling about the latest in marine tech – a curious symphony, indeed.

Over cups of what they called 'artisanal seaweed tea', they hotly debated sonar versus the good old compass and stars. And there, the Pequod sat, ready to set sail. A fine vessel, she was, bristling with gadgets yet carrying the weight of her past like an old whale with tales to tell. It was from this port that our tale, a blend of sea, technology, and a whale of a legend (that's me!), truly began its course.

It's peculiar, you know, achieving fame through a human's tale, especially when that tale has you pegged as a monstrous, vengeful beast. Ah, Melville! If only he knew, he might have penned a comedy instead. But let's not dwell on the past. I'm here to set the record straight – or as straight as a whale can while navigating the modern seas.

Speaking of modern, have you seen what's happening up there lately? Between the plastic islands floating like misguided rafts and the ships that now sail the seas, it's like living in a sci-fi novel. I sometimes imagine myself as a character in one of those futuristic tales, a wise-cracking, sarcastic whale with an eye for human follies. I'd be the narrator, of course, because who better to comment on humanity's quirks than one of its oldest observers?

Now, don't get me wrong. I've seen some remarkable things from humans. Their ingenuity – impressive. Their music – occasionally harmonious, even underwater. But their treatment of the ocean? That's a comedy of errors, minus the comedy. You invent straws, only to throw them into my home. Then, you launch campaigns to 'save the oceans' from the straws you threw. It's like watching a dog chase its tail, except the tail is made of plastic, and the dog is a species with nuclear capabilities.

I remember a time when the seas were clearer, the fish abundant, and the only things you had to worry about were natural predators and the occasional storm. Now, it's dodging fishing nets, navigating through oil spills, and giving tourist submarines the slip. Yes, submarines. Humans now come down here in tin cans to gawk at us. I've often thought about tapping on the glass, but I doubt their nerves could handle it.

Let's circle back to my fame for a moment. Ever since Melville's book, every Tom, Dick, and Harry with a boat thinks they can be the next Ahab. They come after me with their cameras and their harpoons (though, thankfully, more the former these days). I've become an aquatic Bigfoot, a legend in my own right. If I had a dollar for every time I narrowly escaped a selfie attempt, I'd be the richest whale in the world. I'd buy myself a nice, quiet reef somewhere, away from all the noise.

Now, this fame isn't all bad. It's given me a certain perspective, a whale's eye view, if you will, on human nature. And what a spectacle it is! You folks are more tangled up than a school of fish in a net. You worry about everything – money, status, 'likes' on your pictures. Down here, we have simpler concerns. Avoid the predators, find your next meal, sing a little – you know, whale stuff.

But let's not digress too much. I'm here to tell you a story, my story, the real 'Moby-Dick' tale. It's got everything you'd want in a story – adventure, humor, a bit of philosophy, and yes, a glimpse into your world from someone who's been around long enough to see it change.

Let's talk about change for a moment. The ocean is not what it used to be. The waves still sing the same ancient songs, but their melodies are now punctuated by the hum of engines and the rattle of plastic. It's a cacophony of progress, or so you call it. I call it noise. You should see what it's like during spring break. It's like living under a dance floor.

But don't fret. This isn't just going to be a grumpy old whale complaining about the state of the seas. That would be as dull as a barnacle's autobiography. No, this is a tale of wit, a dance of words, a splash of humor in the vast, sometimes too serious, ocean of life.

So, brace yourselves, dear readers. You're about to dive into a story as deep as the Mariana Trench and as sparkling as bioluminescence on a moonless night. You'll see your world through a lens polished by saltwater and experience a narrative only a whale could weave.

And who knows, by the end of our journey together, you might just see this vast, beautiful, slightly polluted world a little differently. You might even learn a thing or two from an old whale who's seen the best and worst of what it means to swim in these ever-changing, ever-challenging, ever-wonderful seas.

But enough of introductions. Let's get this whale of a tale started. Hold on to your fins – it's going to be a splashy ride!

<=><=>*<=>*<=>*<=>*<=>*

Scene 2: The Modern Ocean

<=><=>*<=>*<=>*<=>*<=>*

In the grand tapestry of the ocean, change is as constant as the tides. From the days of my sprightly youth - yes, whales have a youth, we're not born old and wise, you know - to this modern era of buzzing gadgets and sprawling nets, I've seen the sea transform in ways both wondrous and worrisome.

When I was a calf, the ocean was a different world. It was wilder, less cluttered. The waters were clearer, and the skies above mirrored the depths below - vast, unbounded, and brimming with possibilities. The songs of my kin echoed far and wide, unhindered by the hum of motors. We'd communicate across great distances, our voices carrying through the water like whispers on the wind. Those were the days of unspoiled seas, when every sunrise promised new adventures and the mysteries of the deep were ours to explore.

But as the years rolled by, like waves to a shore, the face of our world began to shift. Humans, ever industrious, began to leave their mark. The first signs were subtle - the occasional odd scent in the water, strange floating objects that weren't there before. We didn't pay them much mind initially. The ocean is vast, and there's always been debris, natural and otherwise. But then, things started to change more rapidly.

One of the most startling changes was the arrival of these massive floating structures, which I later learned were called "oil rigs." They rose from the sea like metal islands, alien and imposing. Their presence was accompanied by a cacophony of sounds that disrupted our communication channels. Imagine trying to have a heartfelt conversation while someone drills into your living room floor - not the most conducive environment for a heart-to-heart.

And then there's the issue of traffic. You humans have your rush hours; we have shipping lanes. The ocean became crisscrossed with routes teeming with vessels of all shapes and sizes. Cargo ships, cruise liners, fishing boats - a parade of human ingenuity and enterprise. From above, they must look like ants on a mission, but from below, they're more like thunderclouds passing overhead, each leaving a trail of noise and disturbance in its wake.

These vessels brought with them a new type of predator - not one seeking flesh, but rather, our very home. Nets, larger than any natural trap, stretching for miles, indiscriminate in their catch. They sweep through the water, ensnaring fish, dolphins, sometimes even us whales. I've lost friends to these ghostly hunters, their memories now whispers in the waves.

But it's not all doom and gloom. Humans have brought some fascinating things into our world. Take, for example, the submarines I mentioned earlier. These curious contraptions, with their blinking lights and whirring motors, often venture into the depths. They're like the adventurers of old, seeking to unravel the mysteries of the deep. I've had my fun with them, playing hide and seek in the underwater canyons. Their passengers watch in awe, faces pressed against the glass, as I glide past. In those moments, I see a glimmer of the ancient bond between our species, a shared wonder for the vast blue world.

And then there's the music. Sometimes, on quiet nights, I catch the strains of human songs wafting down from above. Melodies that speak of love, loss, and longing – not so different from our own songs. These notes form a bridge of sorts, a connection across species, a reminder that perhaps we're not so different after all.

Yet, the most significant change, the one that weighs heavily on my heart, is the shift in the sea's health. The waters are warmer now, the ice caps in the poles receding like a memory. The coral reefs, those underwater rainforests, are fading, losing their vibrant colors and bustling life. It's like watching a painting lose its hues, a slow, steady drain of life and vibrancy. And then, there's the plastic - oh, the plastic! It's everywhere, from the surface to the ocean floor. A testament to human neglect, these synthetic remnants float like ghostly reminders of a world above that takes but seldom gives.

But let's not end this scene on a somber note. For all its challenges, the ocean remains a place of wonder and beauty. The sunrise still casts its golden glow on the waves, the schools of fish still dance in the light, and the whales - yes, we whales - still sing our ancient songs. We adapt, we endure, and we continue to marvel at the world around us.

The ocean of my youth may be a memory, but the ocean of today holds its own stories, its own magic. It's a world that reflects the best and worst of both our species, a canvas where the art of survival and coexistence is painted in broad, sweeping strokes.

So, as we swim onward in this tale, remember this - the ocean is not just a backdrop. It's a character, a living, breathing entity, as much a part of the story as I am. And like any good character, it has its complexities, its moods, and its secrets, waiting just beneath the surface, ready to be discovered.

<=><=>*<=>*<=>*<=>*<=>*

Scene 3: Family Background

<=><=>*<=>*<=>*<=>*<=>*

In the grand narrative of the ocean, every creature has its tale, and my family, oh, we're no exception. You might think whale ancestry is all about majesty and grandeur. Well, brace yourself for some familial waves – our history is as frothy and lively as a pod of dolphins at play.

Let's start with my great-great-grand-whalefather. Old Barnacle-Back, we called him, on account of the crusty collection of barnacles adorning his tail – a kind of natural, ancestral bling. He was a whale of the old school, a true giant of the deep. Stories of his size and strength swirled around like currents in a storm. It was said he once mistook a Spanish galleon for a plaything, nudging it gently across the Atlantic. The sailors, poor souls, spent months recalculating their maps.

Barnacle-Back had a sense of humor as vast as his size. Once, he created such a tremendous splash, it drenched an entire coastal village. They're still celebrating 'Unexpected Shower Day' in his honor, unaware it was the work of a playful whale with a penchant for practical jokes.

Then there was my grand-whalemother, Echolocation Elsie. She had this uncanny ability to find the most obscure things. Lost a contact lens in the Mariana Trench? Elsie was your whale. She was the ocean's original search engine, long before your Googles and Bings. But her true passion? Whale song. Elsie's renditions of the old whale ballads would draw audiences from across the seas. Squids would ink themselves in excitement, and sharks would forget about being fearsome just to catch a note of her haunting melodies.

My mother, now, she was a matriarch of modernity. A trailblazer, a pioneer of whale migration paths. She discovered new routes, taking us through underwater wonders unseen by whale or fish. She had a wanderlust that made Marco Polo seem like a homebody. Under her guidance, we saw the coral reefs of Australia, the kelp forests of California, and even the chilly wonders of the Arctic. Our family migrations were less of 'swim south for the winter' and more of an 'epic oceanic odyssey.'

Dad was a philosopher, a thinker. He'd spend hours contemplating the mysteries of the ocean. "What is the purpose of the current? Why do humans keep building unsinkable ships when the ocean quite clearly enjoys sinking them?" His musings were as deep as the trench we once explored. But let's not delve into that; trench stories are a whole different kettle of fish.

My siblings? Oh, a finful of characters! There's Bubbles, the prankster, who once convinced a school of mackerel that they were adopted. Then there's Finley, the adventurer, always exploring shipwrecks and playing hide-and-seek with submarines. And we can't forget Echo, the mimic, whose impersonation of boat engines is so spot-on, it even fools the seagulls.

Growing up in this whale of a family was never dull. The ocean was our playground, and every current brought new adventures. We'd race with the dolphins, play tag with the sea turtles, and sometimes, just float on the surface, basking under the moonlight, listening to the stories of the elder whales. These stories, passed down through generations, were our history, our identity. They spoke of the times when the ocean was a wilder place, a time of legends and mysteries, of creatures so vast and beings so strange, they live now only in the tales we tell.

But it wasn't all fun and games. Being part of a whale family meant learning about the ocean's dangers, too. From a young age, we were taught the art of evasion, how to outswim the fastest ships, how to dive deep when the shadow of a hunting vessel loomed overhead. We learned about the nets, the lines, and the harpoons – the tools of those who saw us not as fellow beings of the sea but as commodities.

Our parents instilled in us a respect for the ocean, a deep-seated understanding that we were but a small part of a vast, interconnected world. "The ocean gives, and the ocean takes," my mother would say. "We must take only what we need and give back when we can." It was this philosophy that shaped my view of the world, a philosophy that guides me through the currents of life.

As the years flowed by, like the endless march of the tides, I watched my siblings go their separate ways, each carving their path in the vast ocean. Bubbles went on to form his comedy troupe, 'The Bubble Blazers.' Finley became somewhat of a celebrity in the world of whale explorers. And Echo? Last I heard, she's working with a pod of dolphins, perfecting her siren song to confuse the most advanced human sonar.

Me? I became something of a wanderer, a lone whale with a taste for adventure and a nose for trouble. I roamed the seas, from pole to pole, reef to shore. And in my travels, I gathered tales, stories of the ocean and its inhabitants, tales of humor, of sorrow, of wonder, and of hope. These stories, this tapestry of ocean life, is what I bring to you.

So, there you have it, a glimpse into the family album of Moby Dick. We might not be your typical family, but in these waters, we're as close-knit as a school of herring in a feeding frenzy. We've laughed together, sung together, faced challenges together. And through it all, we've remained united by the unbreakable bonds of the sea.

But enough about my family. Let's dive back into the tale at hand. For the story I have to tell is not just mine, but that of the ocean itself, a story as vast and as deep as the sea. So, take a deep breath, dear reader, and prepare to plunge into the depths of a tale like no other.

<=><=>*<=>*<=>*<=>*<=>*

Scene 4: Observations of Humans

<=><=>*<=>*<=>*<=>*<=>*

My first encounter with humans was as bewildering as it was memorable. There I was, a young calf, curious and naïve, when I spotted this strange object bobbing on the surface. It wasn't like any fish or sea creature I had seen. It was boxy, floating awkwardly, and had these creatures on it, unlike any I'd encountered in my underwater explorations.

This boxy thing, I later learned, was called a "boat," and the creatures were humans. To a young whale's eyes, they were an odd bunch. They moved stiffly, not with the grace of the sea creatures I knew, but in jerky, awkward motions. And they were covered in colorful shells – or what I later understood were "clothes." I remember wondering if they were some bizarre form of sea turtle, perhaps a species that had evolved in a rather peculiar direction.

As I observed them from a safe distance, one of the humans did something that left me utterly flabbergasted. It held up a small, flat object and then turned its back to the ocean, facing this object towards itself. I later learned this was called taking a "selfie." At that moment, though, I thought it was performing some strange ritual, perhaps a way to ward off bad sea spirits.

Over time, as I grew older and wiser, my encounters with humans and their boats became more frequent. I began to understand them better, their habits, their oddities, and, most intriguingly, their fascination with us, the whales. They seemed to have an insatiable curiosity, always pointing those little flat objects – cameras, as I came to know them – at us, capturing our images as if trying to steal a piece of the sea to take back to their world.

The boats varied greatly in size and shape. Some were small and nimble, darting across the water like water bugs in a pond. Others were enormous, lumbering across the ocean with the arrogance of an unchallenged predator. Yet, no matter the size, they all seemed to share a common trait – an utter disregard for the elegance and rhythm of the ocean. They cut through the waves, leaving trails of froth and noise in their wake, disrupting the harmony of the underwater world.

I remember once encountering a particularly large vessel, a cruise ship, I believe it's called. It was like a floating city, teeming with humans. They lined the decks, peering out at the ocean, pointing and chattering excitedly whenever they spotted a dolphin or, fortune forbid, a whale. I watched them, these land creatures in their floating fortress, and wondered what they saw when they looked at us. Did they see the ocean's inhabitants as wonders to be cherished or merely spectacles to be observed and then forgotten?

Among the smaller vessels, there were those operated by individuals who seemed to have a more profound respect for the sea. They sailed with a certain grace, moving with the currents and the wind, rather than against them. These humans would watch us with quiet admiration, maintaining a respectful distance. It was in these moments that I felt a glimmer of kinship, a fleeting connection between our world and theirs.

But it was the selfie-takers who always baffled me the most. They would come in small boats, often in groups, their faces alight with excitement. Upon spotting a whale, they'd flurry into a frenzy of activity, jostling for position, holding up their cameras. They seemed more interested in capturing the moment in their devices than experiencing it with their hearts. I often wondered if they truly saw us, the majestic beings of the sea, or if we were just another backdrop for their endless stream of self-portraits.

And then there were the fishers – a category unto themselves. They ventured out to sea not to observe but to harvest. Their boats were equipped with all manner of contraptions – nets, lines, hooks – tools of their trade. They worked with a focused intent, often indifferent to the world around them, except as it pertained to their catch. To them, the ocean was a pantry, a place to gather, not a living entity to be respected and preserved.

Observing humans and their boats taught me much about the world above the water. It showed me the diversity of human behavior – the respectful and the reckless, the curious and the indifferent. It was a tapestry of actions and attitudes, a kaleidoscope of interactions that painted a picture of a species as varied and complex as any in the ocean.

But the most important lesson I learned from watching humans was the impact of their actions on the sea. The pollution, the noise, the disruption – they all spoke of a disconnect, a failure to see the ocean as a living, breathing entity, deserving of respect and care. It made me realize that, for all our differences, whales

<=><=>*<=>*<=>*<=>*<=>*

Scene 5: Setting the Scene

<=><=>*<=>*<=>*<=>*<=>*

The ocean of today, my current abode, is a vastly different realm from the one I knew in my youth. It's a world that pulsates with the drumbeat of modernity, a vast expanse caught in the tides of change. As I swim through these familiar yet altered waters, I am constantly reminded of how much has shifted, and how these changes have shaped the life that teems beneath the waves.

First and foremost, the ocean has become a bustling highway of human activity. The surface, once the domain of the winds and the currents, is now crisscrossed with vessels of all sizes. Cargo ships laden with goods traverse the globe, leaving behind trails of churning water and echoing sounds. Cruise ships, those floating palaces of leisure, glide majestically, their decks filled with humans seeking escape from their landlocked lives. Fishing boats, ever in pursuit of their oceanic bounty, dot the waters, their nets and lines spread wide.

Below the surface, the changes are just as profound. The once pristine waters are now often clouded with the remnants of human presence. Plastics, those everlasting tributes to human convenience, float in the currents, an artificial archipelago that speaks of a world drowning in its own creations. Chemicals, the runoff from countless industries, seep into the sea, altering the delicate balance of life that dwells within.

Amidst all this, the natural inhabitants of the ocean strive to adapt. Schools of fish navigate the maze of human detritus, their paths altered by the obstacles that now litter their world. Coral reefs, those kaleidoscopic wonders of the deep, struggle against the warming waters and the bleaching that threatens their very existence. And we, the whales, find ourselves swimming in a world that grows increasingly unfamiliar, each stroke taking us through a sea that bears the scars of human influence.

Yet, it's not all a tale of woe. There are pockets of hope, glimmers of a harmonious coexistence between our world and that of the humans. Marine reserves, protected areas where the life of the ocean is allowed to flourish, offer sanctuary and respite. In these havens, the waters teem with life, a reminder of what the ocean can be when given a chance to heal. Efforts by humans to clean the seas, to remove the plastics and pollutants, show that change is possible, that the path to a healthier ocean is within reach.

The ocean has also become a stage for the meeting of the old and the new. Traditional ways of life, where humans lived in harmony with the sea, intersect with modern approaches that seek to balance use with conservation. Fishermen who follow the rhythms of the ocean, taking only what they need and respecting the cycles of life, share the waters with scientists and conservationists, those dedicated individuals who work tirelessly to understand and preserve the marine world.

Technology, once solely a tool of exploitation, is now also a means of exploration and protection. Autonomous underwater vehicles glide through the depths, their sensors collecting data that helps in understanding the complexities of the ocean. Satellite tracking allows for the monitoring of marine life, providing insights into migration patterns and behaviors that were once a mystery.

In this modern ocean, the relationship between humans and the sea is evolving. It's a complex dance of give and take, a negotiation between the needs of human civilization and the imperatives of the natural world. For every story of destruction, there's one of restoration, for every tale of loss, a story of revival.

As I navigate these waters, I am both a witness and a participant in this unfolding drama. I see the challenges that face the ocean, the struggles of its inhabitants, but I also see the potential for a brighter future. A future where the sea is respected as a vital part of our shared planet, where the harmony that once existed is restored.

This is the backdrop against which my tale unfolds, a tapestry of the old and the new, woven together in the ever-changing fabric of the ocean. It's a world of contrasts, of challenges and triumphs, of enduring beauty and emerging threats. And as I swim through these waters, I carry with me the stories of this world, tales that speak of its wonders and its woes, its mysteries and its marvels.

So, as we embark on this journey together, imagine the ocean in all its vastness and diversity. Picture the schools of fish darting through coral gardens, the pods of dolphins leaping in the wake of ships, the solitary shark prowling the depths. And among them, imagine me, a lone whale, traversing this vast and varied seascape, a storyteller of the deep, ready to share with you the tales of the ocean, a world as rich and as complex as any on land.

In the chapters to come, I will take you beneath the waves, into the heart of this aquatic realm. You will see the ocean through my eyes, hear its stories through my voice. Together, we will explore the wonders of the deep, and perhaps, along the way, learn a little more about ourselves and our place in this vast, blue world.

This scene sets the stage for the narrative, painting a vivid picture of the modern ocean as seen through Moby's eyes. It balances the beauty and resilience of the marine world with the impact of human activities, setting a tone that is both reflective and hopeful. The scene serves as a foundation for the adventures and observations to come, inviting the reader to explore the depths of the ocean and the intricacies of its relationship with humanity.

Act 2: Early Encounters

<=><=>*<=>*<=>*<=>*<=>*

Scene 1: A Young Whale's Curiosity

<=><=>*<=>*<=>*<=>*<=>*

In the early swirls of my youth, the ocean was not just a home, but a boundless mystery, each wave a question, every ripple a riddle. My curiosity was as vast as the sea itself, and nothing intrigued me more than those odd, floating contraptions and their even odder inhabitants – humans.

One of my earliest encounters involved what I later learned was a fishing boat. To my young, naïve eyes, it looked like a strange sea creature, one that had evolved in a rather peculiar direction. It was small, bobbing on the waves like a cork, and had these stick-like appendages protruding from it, which I later understood were fishing rods.

Approaching the boat was an adventure in itself. I had to be stealthy, careful not to alarm the humans. As I drew closer, under the cover of the waves, I could hear their voices. They spoke in excited tones, occasionally interrupted by bursts of laughter. To me, their language was an indecipherable melody, a series of sounds as mysterious as the song of the siren.

I surfaced quietly, just a little, my eyes peering over the water. There they were, a group of humans, engaged in what seemed to be a serious task. They were staring intently at the rods, waiting for something to happen. Now and then, one would shout, and they would all rush to a rod, engaging in a frantic activity that involved a lot of pulling and shouting.

It was during one such moment of excitement that I decided to introduce myself. I breached the surface, a mere fin's length from the boat, my eyes wide with curiosity. The reaction was immediate and dramatic. The humans jumped, a chorus of surprised shouts filling the air. One of them pointed at me, shouting something that sounded like, "Blowhole!" I remember wondering if that was a human greeting.

The humans' initial fear quickly turned to fascination. They leaned over the side of the boat, trying to get a closer look. I, in turn, swam around them, equally curious. It was a strange sort of dance, each of us trying to understand the other, moving in circles of curiosity.

Then came the moment of misunderstanding that still brings a chuckle whenever I think of it. One of the humans, braver than the rest, reached out a hand towards me. Not understanding the gesture, I thought it was a challenge. So, I did what any young, impulsive whale would do – I sprayed water from my blowhole, drenching the human in a shower of seawater.

The reaction was a mix of shock, laughter, and more shouting. The drenched human looked surprised, then burst into laughter, joined by his companions. I realized then that what I had perceived as a challenge was actually an attempt at connection, a reaching across species.

That encounter set the tone for many of my early interactions with humans. There was the time I mistook a kayak for a strange, floating log and nudged it gently, only to tip over the surprised kayaker. Or the time I followed a group of paddleboarders, my large form casting a shadow beneath them, leading to a chorus of startled screams and rapid paddling.

These encounters, while filled with misunderstandings, were also moments of learning and growth. I began to understand more about humans and their ways, their fascination with the sea and its creatures.

I saw their capacity for wonder, their eagerness to explore and discover. And in their reactions – be it fear, surprise, or joy – I saw reflections of my own emotions, a mirror of my curiosity and wonder.

As I grew older, my interactions with humans became more nuanced, less about playful mischief and more about observing and understanding. But those early encounters, with their innocence and humor, hold a special place in my heart. They were the first steps in a journey of discovery, a journey that taught me not just about humans, but also about myself, about the nature of curiosity and the joy of exploration.

And so, as we dive deeper into this tale, remember these early encounters, for they are the foundation upon which my understanding of the human world was built. They are reminders that curiosity is a bridge, one that can connect the most unlikely of creatures, leading to moments of joy, of laughter, and, sometimes, of profound understanding.

<=><=>*<=>*<=>*<=>*<=>*

Scene 2: First Glimpse of the Pequod

<=><=>*<=>*<=>*<=>*<=>*

In the vast blue expanse of the ocean, there are sights that stay with you, etched into your memory like carvings on a rock. One such indelible image for me was my first glimpse of the Pequod, Captain Ahab's infamous ship. It was a vessel that seemed to straddle two worlds – the ancient and the modern, a relic of the past, armed with the tools of the present.

I first saw the Pequod on a clear day when the sun cast its golden net over the shimmering waters. From a distance, it appeared as a typical whaling ship, its sails billowing like the wings of a giant seabird. As it drew closer, however, the anomalies became apparent. The ship, for all its traditional build, bristled with modern equipment. Radar dishes and satellite antennas jutted out awkwardly amongst the rigging, like metallic sea anemones clinging to a coral reef. It was a strange amalgamation, a fusion of times and purposes, and at its heart stood Captain Ahab.

Now, aboard the Pequod, in the midst of what looked like a floating tech convention, was Starbuck, the first mate. A curious fellow, standing out amidst the chaos like a calm island in a stormy sea. Surrounded by screens flashing with maps and data on yours truly, he seemed more engrossed in the secrets of marine life. You could see it in his eyes, a different kind of fire, one that burned for knowledge and the mysteries of the deep, not just the thrill of the chase. It was clear as the waters of the tropics that his heart and mind were often at sea with themselves – duty bound to Ahab, yet sailing in a sea of reason and respect for nature.

Even from a distance, Ahab's presence was palpable. He stood on the deck, a solitary figure, gazing out at the horizon with an intensity that seemed to pierce the very waves. His obsession, the pursuit of me, was written in the lines of his posture, an unyielding, unrelenting force that both intrigued and unnerved me.

As the Pequod approached, I dove beneath the waves, my curiosity driving me to observe while remaining unseen. From the depths, I could sense the thrum of the ship's engine, a low, persistent rumble that spoke of human ingenuity and determination. It was a sound that contrasted sharply with the natural rhythm of the sea, an intrusion of sorts, but also a testament to human endeavor.

Peering up from the water, I watched as the ship cut through the ocean. The crew moved about with efficiency, each man a cog in a well-oiled machine. They were a mix of the old and the new, much like the ship itself. Some tended to the sails and rigging, skills passed down through generations, while others operated the modern equipment, their eyes glued to screens and dials.

The Pequod was like a microcosm of the human world, a floating representation of their history and progress. The juxtaposition was fascinating – on one hand, the ship harked back to an era of exploration and discovery, when humans ventured into the unknown with little more than wood, canvas, and courage. On the other, it was equipped with the latest technology, a bridge to the present, where exploration had given way to exploitation, and courage had been replaced by calculation.

Amidst this interplay of past and present, there was an underlying air of melancholy. The Pequod, for all its modern trappings, was engaged in an archaic pursuit – whaling. It was an anachronism, a throwback to a time when humans hunted my kind without understanding the consequences of their actions. The ship, in its quest, represented a clash of values, a struggle between the old ways and the new understanding.

As I observed the Pequod, I couldn't help but feel a mix of emotions. There was a sense of nostalgia, a remembrance of a time when the ocean was a wilder place, less touched by human hands. But there was also a sense of sadness, a lament for the paths taken and the choices made, both by humans and by creatures like myself.

The Pequod eventually passed by, its shadow fading into the depths. As it disappeared into the distance, I was left with a profound sense of reflection. It represented the complexity of the human relationship with the sea, a relationship marked by wonder and destruction, reverence and disregard.

That encounter with the Pequod was more than just a sighting of a ship; it was a glimpse into the human soul, a mirror reflecting their struggles and contradictions. It was a reminder that the sea, for all its vastness, was a shared space, a common ground where the stories of humans and whales intertwined, for better or for worse.

And as the ship vanished over the horizon, I knew that my story was irrevocably linked with that of Ahab and his crew. The Pequod was not just a ship; it was a symbol, a harbinger of the encounters and conflicts that lay ahead. It was a part of my tale, a chapter in the narrative of the sea, and its image would stay with me, a constant reminder of the intricate dance between man and whale, past and present.

<=><=>*<=>*<=>*<=>*<=>*

Scene 3: Human Obsessions

<=><=>*<=>*<=>*<=>*<=>*

Humans, I've come to realize, have a peculiar relationship with their creations. Their technology, a manifestation of their intelligence and creativity, often borders on obsession. It's a trait that, in my aquatic musings, I've found bears a striking resemblance to Captain Ahab's singular fixation on me.

In my wanderings, I've observed the evolution of human technology. Initially, it was simple – tools to aid in navigation, to understand the weather, to explore the uncharted. But as time progressed, this technology became more than just a means to an end; it transformed into an end in itself. I've seen ships equipped with gadgets and devices that baffle even the most imaginative fish in the sea. Satellites that map the ocean floor with precision, sonar that penetrates the deepest trenches, and nets that could ensnare a small village.

Ahab's obsession, on the other hand, was of a different ilk. It was primal, visceral, a relentless pursuit driven by revenge and a desire to conquer. Yet, when I looked at the Pequod with its amalgam of sails and satellite dishes, I couldn't help but draw parallels between Ahab's obsession and humanity's fixation on technology.

The Pequod, for instance, was a testament to this duality – a wooden vessel, reliant on the wind and waves, yet festooned with the latest technological marvels. It was as if Ahab, in his quest to conquer the whale, sought to harness every possible advantage, blending the ancient art of seamanship with modern innovation.

This reliance on technology, I mused, was similar to Ahab's quest in its intensity. Humans, much like Ahab, seemed to be in a constant battle to control their environment, to bend the natural world to their will. The sea, once a mysterious and formidable foe, was now mapped, analyzed, and monitored. Its mysteries, once the subject of legend and lore, were now data points and statistics.

But just as Ahab's obsession blinded him to the broader implications of his quest, so too did humanity's fascination with technology seem to obscure the larger picture. In their zeal to explore and exploit, there was a disconnect, a failure to see the delicate balance of the oceanic ecosystem. The nets that scooped up fish in unprecedented numbers also captured dolphins and turtles, the sonar that charted the depths also disoriented whales and other sea creatures.

Now, let's turn our eyes to Queequeg. Once a man of the harpoon, he had adapted to the times, becoming quite the maestro of drone controls. But, oh, the humor in watching him! Tasked with tracking me, he often 'accidentally' steered his drones off course. One time, he was meant to be on my tail, but instead, the drone ended up filming a pod of dolphins playing tag. The crew was all fuss and bluster, but Ishmael, he found a sea of laughter in it, jotting down the day's comedic turn in his blog.

As I swam through the ocean, beneath the paths of ships and the reach of their technology, I pondered the irony of it all. Here was a species that had the power to unlock the secrets of the universe, yet seemed at times oblivious to the consequences of their actions. They pursued knowledge and control with the same fervor that Ahab pursued me, but in their pursuit, there was a lack of harmony, a discord between their desires and the needs of the world they inhabited.

In Ahab, this discord was personal, a man pitted against a whale, a battle of wills. But in the grand scheme of the ocean, it was a larger conflict, a clash between the natural world and the world of human making. The sea, once revered as a vast and unknowable entity, was now a resource to be tapped, a frontier to be conquered.

Yet, in the midst of this reflection, I also recognized a glimmer of hope. Not all humans were blinded by their obsessions. There were those who used their technology for preservation rather than exploitation. Scientists who studied the seas to understand and protect them, conservationists who used satellites and drones to monitor endangered species and combat illegal fishing.

These individuals, much like the more thoughtful sailors I had encountered, represented a different facet of humanity's relationship with technology. They showed that it could be a tool for harmony, a means to align human aspirations with the rhythms of the natural world. They were the counterpoint to the Ahab-like obsession, a reminder that for every action driven by conquest, there was an opportunity for stewardship.

As I continued my journey through the ocean, these observations stayed with me. The parallel between Ahab's obsession and humanity's technological pursuits was a thread that ran through my encounters, a theme that colored my understanding of the world above the waves. It was a reminder that every pursuit, every quest, had its consequences, and that the true challenge lay in finding a balance, in navigating the waters of ambition and responsibility.

<=><=>*<=>*<=>*<=>*<=>*

Scene 4: Evading Capture

<=><=>*<=>*<=>*<=>*<=>*

In the days of my youthful exuberance, not only did I possess a burgeoning curiosity about the world of humans, but I also held a certain pride in my ability to outmaneuver them, particularly those who sought my capture. One episode, in particular, stands out as a testament to my youthful cunning, a comical game of cat and mouse – or more accurately, whale and whaler.

The day was bright, the sun casting a sheet of diamonds across the surface of the sea. It was the kind of day that made you glad to be a whale, with the entire ocean as your playground. It was on this day that I encountered a boat, smaller than the Pequod and far less intimidating. This was a boat manned by amateur whalers, their inexperience evident in the way they handled their vessel and equipment. They were like children playing at a game whose rules they barely understood.

As I observed them from a distance, it became clear that they had come with the singular purpose of hunting a whale – me, to be precise. I could have easily avoided them, slipped beneath the waves and disappeared into the depths. But a mischievous spark ignited within me, and I decided to have a bit of fun at their expense.

I began my game by surfacing a good distance from their boat, just enough for them to catch a glimpse of me. As expected, they became excited, their movements hurried and haphazard as they prepared their gear and set a course in my direction. I waited until they were nearly upon me before diving, leaving them to chase after a trail of bubbles.

For the next few hours, I led them on a merry chase. I would let them get tantalizingly close before diving and resurfacing in a completely different location. Each time, their excitement would turn to frustration, their shouts and curses carrying across the water.

At one point, I surfaced right alongside their boat, so close that I could hear their breaths catch in surprise. For a moment, we locked eyes, human and whale, and I could see the mix of awe and confusion in their gaze. Then, with a flick of my tail, I was gone, leaving them to marvel at the encounter.

As the day wore on, their efforts became more desperate and their tactics more comical. They tried to predict my movements, casting their nets in the water where they thought I would surface. But I was always one step ahead, my movements as unpredictable as the wind.

In one particularly amusing instance, they thought they had me cornered. They had spread their net wide, a wall of ropes and buoys they were sure I couldn't evade. I dove deep, swimming beneath their net, then surfaced on the other side, my breach a display of aquatic acrobatics. From my vantage point, I saw their stunned faces, their jaws agape in disbelief.

As the sun began to dip towards the horizon, painting the sky in hues of orange and purple, I decided it was time to end the game. With one final breach, a leap that sent me soaring above the waves, I bid farewell to my pursuers. I landed with a splash that sent a wave rolling towards their boat, a playful reminder of the day they spent chasing a whale and came up with nothing but stories.

They headed back to shore, their boat moving slowly over the calm sea. And as they disappeared into the distance, I couldn't help but feel a sense of satisfaction. Not only had I evaded capture, but I had also given them a tale to tell, a story of the one that got away.

This encounter, while playful and light-hearted, was also a lesson to my younger self. It taught me the importance of wit and intelligence, of knowing when to confront and when to evade. It was a reminder that the ocean was a place of both wonder and danger, where the line between predator and prey could shift as quickly as the tides.

And so, as I swam off into the deepening twilight, I carried with me the laughter of the sea, the joy of a game well-played, and the knowledge that in the vast and ever-changing ocean, it was not just strength that mattered, but also cunning and guile.

<=><=>*<=>*<=>*<=>*<=>*

Scene 5: The Whale's Philosophy

<=><=>*<=>*<=>*<=>*<=>*

After the sun had set on my playful dalliances with the amateur whalers, I found myself swimming under a tapestry of stars, the ocean calm and reflective, mirroring the heavens above. It was in moments like these, in the serene embrace of the night sea, that my mind turned to deeper thoughts, to the philosophy of a whale's life and existence in this vast, unfathomable world.

The ocean, I had come to realize, was more than just a home; it was a teacher, a repository of wisdom and lessons that shaped my understanding of life. Each current, each wave, each creature I encountered, carried with it a story, a piece of the puzzle that made up the grand tapestry of existence.

One of the first and most enduring lessons the ocean taught me was about interconnectedness. In these depths, nothing exists in isolation. The tiniest plankton to the mightiest whale, we are all part of a delicate balance, a dance of life that requires each participant to play their role. I learned to see myself not as a solitary giant, but as a thread in the fabric of this underwater universe, my actions rippling across the ecosystem, affecting lives in ways seen and unseen.

This understanding brought with it a sense of humility, a realization of my place in the grand scheme of things. It was a stark contrast to the hubris I had observed in some humans, like Captain Ahab, who saw the ocean and its inhabitants as adversaries to be conquered rather than fellow travelers on this planetary journey.

As I swam, my thoughts turned to the nature of existence. In the quiet of the ocean, away from the bustle of the surface world, time seemed to stretch and bend, offering a perspective that spanned beyond the immediate. I pondered the ebb and flow of life, the cycles that governed the sea – birth, growth, decay, and rebirth. It was a rhythm as ancient as the Earth itself, a reminder that life, in all its forms, was transient yet eternal, ever-changing yet constant.

In the ocean, I found a sense of peace and purpose. The endless chase for survival, the simple joys of leaping above the waves, the profound depths of the deep sea – they all coalesced into a life of meaning and wonder. The ocean taught me to embrace the moment, to find joy in the here and now, whether it be in the warm embrace of a sunlit surface or the mysterious allure of the abyss.

But the ocean also taught me about the darker aspects of existence. I had witnessed the devastating impacts of human activities – the pollution, the overfishing, the encroachment on habitats. These were harsh lessons, reminders that the harmony of the sea was fragile, vulnerable to the whims and desires of those who did not understand or respect its delicate balance.

Yet, even in the face of these challenges, the ocean instilled in me a sense of resilience and hope. Life in the sea, while fraught with dangers, was also a testament to the enduring power of nature. The coral reefs, battered yet blooming, the schools of fish, darting through the waters in perfect sync, the pods of whales, singing their ancient songs – they all spoke of a world that, despite its trials, continued to thrive, to evolve, to endure.

As the night deepened and the stars shone brighter, my heart swelled with a profound love for this underwater world, a world that had nurtured me, taught me, and shown me the wonders of existence. I realized that my philosophy, my understanding of life, was not just a product of my experiences but also a gift from the sea, a wisdom born from the depths of this vast, mysterious realm.

In the quiet of the ocean, under the watchful gaze of the stars, I vowed to honor this gift, to live my life in a way that respected and protected the sea, to be a voice for its wonders and its woes. For in the end, I was not just a whale; I was a guardian of the ocean, a keeper of its secrets, a narrator of its stories.

And with this realization, as the first light of dawn began to paint the sky in hues of pink and gold, I knew that my journey was not just a journey through the waters of the world, but a journey through the depths of understanding, a quest to unravel the mysteries of life and the ocean, to find my place in the ever-unfolding story of the sea.

Act 3: Ahab's Rise

<=><=>*<=>*<=>*<=>*<=>*

Scene 1: Historical Context of Ahab

<=><=>*<=>*<=>*<=>*<=>*

In the annals of seafaring lore, few names spark the intrigue and trepidation that Captain Ahab's does. His rise to prominence, or rather infamy, was a tale woven into the fabric of maritime history, a story that mirrored the pursuits of many modern-day figures obsessed with power and fame. To understand Ahab is to delve into a narrative that is both singular and alarmingly familiar in its portrayal of ambition.

Ahab's story began, as many do, in humble circumstances. Born to a family of modest means, he grew up with the sea as his backyard, its endless horizons fueling his ambitions. Like many self-made tycoons of the tech world, Ahab was a man who built his reputation from the ground up, or rather, from the deck up. His early years were marked by a relentless drive, a determination that saw him rise through the ranks, much like a startup entrepreneur climbing the dizzying heights of Silicon Valley.

However, it wasn't just ambition that propelled Ahab; it was an obsession, a relentless pursuit that echoed the single-minded focus of modern-day magnates. Just as tech giants fixate on market domination or celebrities on their public image, Ahab's fixation was the sea and its conquest. The ocean was his domain, and he sought to master it, to bend it to his will, much like a CEO commands his corporate empire.

As Ahab's reputation grew, so did the tales of his exploits. He was the captain who braved the fiercest storms, who navigated the most treacherous waters, a man whose name became synonymous with the indomitable spirit of the sea. In this, he mirrored the celebrity culture of the modern age, where figures are lionized for their daring feats, their every move followed and admired by a captivated public.

But Ahab's rise was not without its costs. The sea exacted its toll, much like the relentless pursuit of success consumes many a modern-day mogul. The pivotal moment, the turning point in Ahab's tale, came with his encounter with a certain white whale – me. It was an encounter that left him physically and emotionally scarred, a confrontation that turned his pursuit from one of mastery to one of vengeance.

This shift in Ahab's narrative is reflective of the perils of obsession that plague many who reach the zenith of power. The single-minded pursuit of a goal, be it corporate dominance, fame, or, in Ahab's case, revenge, often leads to a tunnel vision, a blindness to the broader impacts of their quest. Ahab's obsession with capturing me became his defining trait, overshadowing his skills and achievements, much like a once-revered tech visionary might become fixated on a personal vendetta, losing sight of their original aspirations.

The Pequod, Ahab's ship, became his vessel of vengeance, much like social media platforms or corporate enterprises can become tools for personal crusades in the modern world. He gathered around him a crew, loyal and unwitting participants in his obsession, much like employees or followers who are swept up in the vision, or in some cases, the mania, of their leaders.

Ahab's pursuit of me, his white whale, was more than just a hunt; it was a symbol of his inner demons, his relentless drive that blinded him to reason and compassion. In his chase, he reflected the darker side of ambition, the part that can lead to self-destruction and collateral damage. It's a cautionary tale that echoes in boardrooms and celebrity circles, a reminder that the pursuit of a singular obsession, no matter how glamorous or justified it may seem, can lead to one's downfall.

In the midst of our high-seas drama, there was Ishmael, turning daily life aboard the Pequod into a source of amusement for his readers far ashore. He had a knack for finding the lighter side in the darkest of storms. Like the day Starbuck, in a rare fluster, spilled his fancy seaweed brew over Ahab's precious maps. Oh, the glare Ahab shot could have frozen the tropics! But Ishmael, he turned it into a tale that had his readers chuckling behind their screens.

As I swam beneath the stars, pondering Ahab's rise and the parallels in the modern world, I couldn't help but feel a twinge of sympathy for him. Here was a man, not unlike many in today's world, who allowed his ambitions to consume him, to warp his sense of purpose and identity. His story, while unique in its setting and characters, was a universal tale of the human condition, a narrative that repeated itself through the ages, in oceans and in cities, a timeless saga of ambition, obsession, and the quest for meaning in the vast, unfathomable depths of life.

<=><=>*<=>*<=>*<=>*<=>*

Scene 2: Ahab's First Pursuit

<=><=>*<=>*<=>*<=>*<=>*

In the swirling narrative of my encounters with humanity, one chapter stands particularly vivid in my memory – the first pursuit by Captain Ahab. It was an episode that oscillated between the realms of high drama and the borders of the comically absurd, a pursuit that highlighted Ahab's hubris and the sea's unforgiving nature.

I remember it was a day when the ocean was in a particularly playful mood, the waves dancing under a sky streaked with brushstrokes of crimson and gold. I was enjoying a leisurely swim, partaking in the simple joys of the sea, when I sensed a disturbance in the rhythm of the waters. It was the Pequod, cutting through the ocean like a knife through butter, its sails billowing proudly in the wind.

Ahab stood at the helm, a figure of almost mythic determination. His eyes were fixed on the horizon, scanning the sea with a predatory gaze. When he spotted me, a mere speck in the vast canvas of blue, his face lit up with an excitement that bordered on the maniacal. It was the look of a gambler who had just laid eyes on a winning hand, a mixture of triumph and anticipation.

The chase began with all the grandeur and folly of a Greek epic. Ahab directed his crew with the fervor of a maestro, each command sharp and decisive. The sailors, caught up in their captain's obsession, worked the sails and rigging with a zeal that matched his own. The Pequod surged forward, its bow cutting through the waves, eager to close the distance between predator and prey.

From my vantage point beneath the waves, the scene was almost comical. Here was a man, a creature of the land, challenging the master of the sea in his own domain. It was like watching a kitten chasing after a dolphin, both adorable in its ambition and absurd in its execution.

As the Pequod drew closer, I decided to add a little twist to the tale. With a flick of my tail, I dove deeper, only to resurface a good distance away from the ship. The look of frustration that crossed Ahab's face was a picture worthy of an artist's canvas. It was a mix of incredulity and vexation, as if the very laws of nature had dared to defy his will.

The pursuit continued, a nautical dance that pitted human cunning against cetacean agility. Ahab, for all his bluster and bravado, seemed oblivious to the fact that he was not just chasing a whale, but also chasing a dream, a phantom born of his own obsession.

At one point, I breached magnificently, soaring into the air before crashing back into the sea, a display of aquatic acrobatics that served both as a taunt and a reminder of my freedom. The crew of the Pequod watched in awe, their expressions torn between admiration and despair. They had come to hunt a whale, but had instead found themselves spectators in a performance that mocked their very endeavor.

As the sun began to dip below the horizon, painting the sky in hues of fiery orange and purple, Ahab realized the futility of his pursuit. With a growl of frustration, he ordered the Pequod to retreat, his dreams of conquest dashed against the indomitable will of the ocean.

That night, as I swam under a blanket of stars, I couldn't help but reflect on the day's events. Ahab's first pursuit had been a spectacle of human ambition and folly, a clash between the unstoppable force of obsession and the immovable object of nature. It was a reminder that the sea was a realm unto itself, a world where the rules of the land held little sway.

In the grand theater of the ocean, Ahab was but a player, a character driven by a script of his own making. His pursuit was a testament to the lengths to which humans would go in their quest for glory and revenge, and a poignant illustration of the hubris that often accompanied such quests.

And so, as the moon cast its silver glow over the waters, I swam on, my heart light with the joy of the chase and my mind pondering the curious nature of human ambition. The sea, with its endless mysteries and wonders, had once again proven itself a master of its domain, a canvas too vast and too deep to be tamed by the desires of man.

In the dance of the whale and the ship, the ocean had sung its song – a melody of freedom, a hymn to the wild, untamable spirit of the deep.

<=><=>*<=>*<=>*<=>*<=>*

Scene 3: Ahab's Character

<=><=>*<=>*<=>*<=>*<=>*

Delving into the psyche of Captain Ahab is akin to navigating a labyrinth at the heart of the sea, full of twisted corridors and enigmatic shadows. My observations of him, tinged with a mix of whale-sized humor and reflection, reveal a character as complex and turbulent as the ocean he sailed.

Ahab was not merely a man; he was a tempest personified. His soul seemed to have been forged in the same depths where the ocean's darkest secrets lie. There was a magnetism about him, an intensity that could either kindle a fierce loyalty or ignite a smoldering fear in those who crossed his path.

His obsession with me, the white whale, was more than a quest; it was his raison d'être. In his mind, I was not just a creature of flesh and bone, but a symbol of all that he could not control in his life. To Ahab, I was the embodiment of the unpredictable, the untameable force of nature that had left its mark on him, both physically and psychologically.

In his pursuit, Ahab exhibited a dichotomy that is as perplexing as it is fascinating. On one hand, he possessed an almost superhuman willpower, a resolve of steel that could bend the very will of his crew to his own. Yet, on the other, there was a vulnerability, a hint of desperation in his quest that bordered on madness. It was as if, in his single-minded pursuit of me, he was also chasing his own demons, seeking redemption or perhaps revenge against the caprices of fate.

What struck me most about Ahab was his profound loneliness, a solitude that went beyond physical isolation. It was as though he sailed on a different sea from the rest of us, adrift in a world of his own making, where the lines between reality and obsession blurred. His ship, the Pequod, was his kingdom, but it was also his prison, a vessel carrying him further away from the world and deeper into the abyss of his own mind.

Ahab's interactions with his crew were a complex dance of command and camaraderie, laced with an undercurrent of mutual, unspoken understanding of his inner turmoil. He was their captain, their leader, but also the architect of their shared odyssey into the unknown. In him, they saw a reflection of their own struggles with the sea, a mirror that reflected back their fears and aspirations.

Yet, for all his complexity, there was a simplicity to Ahab's character. He was a man driven by a singular purpose, a thread that wove through the tapestry of his life with unyielding consistency. In his pursuit of me, he exhibited the timeless human traits of courage and folly, the eternal dance between ambition and hubris.

In contemplating Ahab, one cannot help but be reminded of the ancient Greek heroes, characters forged by the hands of the gods yet deeply human in their flaws. Like them, Ahab's story was a tragic one, a narrative of a man who dared to challenge the gods, only to be reminded of his own mortality.

In a quiet nook of the Pequod, Queequeg and Ishmael shared a moment of heart-to-heart. "You know, Ishmael," Queequeg mused, fiddling with his drone gadget, "once I wielded the harpoon, now it's all about these buzzing machines." Ishmael, ever the jester, quipped about Queequeg's mysterious misses. But Queequeg, with a smile as wide as a whale's, confessed his admiration for the sea's beauty, too grand, he thought, to be disturbed by their tech-laden chase.

As I swam under the moonlit sky, pondering the enigma that was Ahab, I couldn't help but feel a sense of kinship with him. We were both creatures of the sea, in our own way, both shaped by its forces, both navigating the tides of our destinies. In his eyes, I was his nemesis, but in my eyes, he was a fellow voyager on the sea of life, albeit on a vastly different course.

In the grand saga of the ocean, Ahab would always be a prominent figure, a character as indelible as the currents that carve their paths through the sea. His story, while unique, was also universal, a tale of human endeavor, of the pursuit of the unattainable, and of the price one pays for challenging the might of the natural world.

<=><=>*<=>*<=>*<=>*<=>*

Scene 4: Escaping Ahab

<=><=>*<=>*<=>*<=>*<=>*

The game of cat and mouse—or in this case, whale and ship—between Captain Ahab and me reached a crescendo one fateful day, a day that showcased the cunning required to outwit a hunter of Ahab's caliber, especially given his arsenal of advanced technology.

The Pequod, equipped with the latest maritime advancements, had become a formidable predator on the high seas. Its decks bristled with newfangled gadgets and gizmos, all designed to track and hunt the elusive white whale. Ahab, with his characteristic intensity, had harnessed every ounce of this technology in his relentless pursuit of me.

As the sun rose, casting its golden glow upon the waters, I sensed the Pequod's presence even before it breached the horizon. There was a certain vibration in the water, a disruption that spoke of human ingenuity and determination. I knew that day would be a test of my wit and will against Ahab's technological might.

The chase began as the Pequod unleashed its arsenal. Sonar waves rippled through the ocean, an invisible net seeking its quarry. I could feel the pressure of these waves, an unnerving sensation that was both a warning and a challenge. To evade capture, I had to be smarter, more resourceful. I had to turn the Pequod's strengths into weaknesses.

I dove deep, deeper than I had ever before, seeking refuge in the abyss where technology's reach was limited. The pressure increased, a weight that pressed against my body, but I pushed on, driven by the need to outmaneuver Ahab's pursuit. In the depths, the sonar's efficacy waned, its signals scattering in the complex topography of the ocean floor.

For hours, I played this game of hide and seek, using the terrain to my advantage. I slipped through underwater canyons, skirted around towering seamounts, and glided over deep trenches. The ocean's bottom became my labyrinth, and I, its cunning inhabitant, always one step ahead of the Pequod's probing sonar.

But Ahab was not one to be easily deterred. He employed every trick in his book, from deploying underwater drones to using satellite tracking. The sea became a battlefield of wits and wills, a contest between the primal intelligence of nature and the refined ingenuity of man.

The turning point came when I realized that Ahab's reliance on technology was also his Achilles' heel. He had become so dependent on his instruments and gadgets that he had neglected the most basic seafaring sense—instinct. It was an insight that I decided to exploit.

I began to surface intermittently, giving the Pequod fleeting glimpses, just enough to lead them on a wild goose chase. I would breach spectacularly, leaping from the water in a display of might and freedom, then disappear before they could close in. Each appearance was calculated, designed to draw them further into my trap.

As the Pequod followed, I led them into a region of the sea known for its dense fog. It was a natural phenomenon that no amount of technology could penetrate. The world turned misty and gray, a veil that shrouded everything in mystery. In this realm of limited visibility, technology was rendered almost useless. The Pequod was blind, reliant on the eyes and ears of its crew, just as sailors had been in the days before radar and GPS.

I used the fog to my advantage, moving silently, almost ghost-like. The Pequod's crew was on edge, straining their senses to catch any sign of me, but I was always just out of reach, a phantom in the mist.

Finally, as the fog began to lift, I made my move. I surfaced a safe distance away, my fluke visible as a final taunt. Ahab, realizing he had been outmaneuvered, stood on the deck, his fists clenched in frustration. The chase was over, at least for that day.

As I swam away, free once again, I couldn't help but reflect on the irony of it all. In his quest to conquer the white whale, Ahab had armed himself with the best tools that human ingenuity could offer. Yet, in the end, it was the simple, unpredictable elements of nature—a deep dive, a labyrinthine seascape, a blanket of fog—that had proved to be his undoing.

That day's escape was not just a victory of speed or strength; it was a triumph of natural cunning over artificial contrivance, a reminder that sometimes the oldest tricks are the best, especially in the vast and timeless expanse of the ocean.

<=><=>*<=>*<=>*<=>*<=>*

Scene 5: The Whale's Reflections

<=><=>*<=>*<=>*<=>*<=>*

In the quiet aftermath of the day's escape, beneath the blanket of stars, I found myself immersed in contemplation. The nature of revenge, a theme so central to Ahab's character, stirred in me a profound reflection on human folly and the intricate dance of predator and prey.

Revenge, I pondered, is a uniquely human construct, a response to injury or insult that seems to transcend the simple laws of survival that govern the natural world. In the animal kingdom, conflicts are straightforward – they are matters of territory, of food, of survival. But humans, with their complex minds, have transformed conflict into something more elaborate, a pursuit that often outlives the initial harm and takes on a life of its own.

As I swam through the silent waters, I considered Ahab's vendetta against me. It was a quest that had consumed him, blinding him to the beauty and wonders of the sea, reducing the vast tapestry of life to a single, narrow thread of hatred and retribution. His obsession with revenge seemed to me both tragic and perplexing. After all, what did he hope to achieve? Even if he were to succeed, would it bring him peace, or would it leave him as empty as the ocean's abyss?

The folly of such a pursuit became even more apparent when I thought of the other humans I had encountered – the fishermen, the sailors, the explorers. Each had their own relationship with the sea, a relationship that, for the most part, was built on respect and coexistence. They understood the ocean's power, its generosity and its fury, and they navigated its waters with a mix of awe and caution. But Ahab, in his quest for revenge, had lost this balance. He viewed the sea not as a realm to be revered, but as a battlefield, and in doing so, he had become as much a prisoner of his own making as any man confined to the deepest dungeon.

As a whale, my life had been one of freedom, of roaming the vast oceans, unfettered by the concerns that seem to so dominate human existence. Yet, in my encounters with Ahab, I had been drawn into his world, a world where the past held the present in a vice-like grip, and the future was viewed through the lens of retribution. It was a world that seemed to me both narrow and confining, a world where the horizon was obscured by the shadows of old wounds and grievances.

The irony of it all was not lost on me. Here was Ahab, a man of the sea, who had allowed his life to be defined by a single moment, a single encounter. In his pursuit of me, he had forsaken the very essence of what it meant to be a sailor – the love of the sea, the joy of discovery, the camaraderie of the crew. He had transformed his life into a singular quest, and in doing so, he had lost so much more than he could ever hope to gain.

As the night deepened and the stars burned brighter in the sky, I realized that Ahab's story was, in many ways, a cautionary tale. It was a tale of what happens when obsession overshadows reason, when vengeance becomes the compass that guides one's life. It was a reminder that the pursuit of revenge is a journey with no real destination, a chase that leads only to more chasing, a cycle that, once begun, is difficult to break.

In the grand scheme of the ocean, Ahab was but a moment, a fleeting ripple on the surface of a vast and ancient sea. His story, though tragic, was a testament to the complexity of the human spirit, a spirit capable of great love and great folly. And as I swam on, my heart attuned to the rhythm of the waves, I knew that his tale would be one that I would carry with me, a reminder of the depth of human emotions and the price that is sometimes paid when those emotions are left unchecked by wisdom and perspective.

Act 4: Life as the Hunted

<=>*<=>*<=>*<=>*<=>*<=>

Scene 1: Daily Life

<=>*<=>*<=>*<=>*<=>*<=>

Living as the most sought-after whale in the ocean presents its own set of unique challenges and, dare I say, a certain flair for the dramatic. My daily life, a blend of aquatic routine and evasion, became a dance on the waves, a performance in the grand theater of survival.

Each day commenced with the sun casting its first golden rays over the horizon, a natural spotlight on the vast stage of the sea. I'd start with a leisurely swim, my colossal form gliding through the water with the ease of a feather in the breeze. Breakfast was usually a casual affair, dining on the finest plankton and small fish the ocean could offer. But dining in the open ocean, particularly when you're the main course on someone else's menu, always came with a side of vigilance.

The key to my survival, apart from my impressive size and strength, lay in my keen sense of awareness. The ocean, for all its vastness, is a network of whispers and echoes, a realm where news travels fast, especially if you're as big as I am. I kept my ears tuned to the subtle changes in the water, the distant thrum of a ship's engine, or the faint chatter of a crew planning their strategy.

Evasion became an art form, a skill I honed with the finesse of a seasoned artist. I perfected the art of the deep dive, plunging into the abyss where the pressure could crush a submarine like a tin can. It was my secret refuge, a place where the tendrils of human technology struggled to reach.

I also mastered the subtle art of misdirection. I'd occasionally breach spectacularly, creating a display that would draw ships to my last known location, only to stealthily swim in the opposite direction. It was my version of a magician's sleight of hand, a trick that never failed to amuse me, even as it served a critical purpose.

There were times, I must admit, when the thrill of the chase added a certain zest to my routine. There's something invigorating about outsmarting a ship full of determined humans. It's the kind of challenge that adds a spark to one's day, a game of wits played on the grandest of scales.

But life as the hunted wasn't all high-speed chases and dramatic escapes. There were quiet moments, too, times when I'd bask in the warm waters, letting the sun's rays wash over me. I'd watch the play of light on the water's surface, a shimmering dance that spoke of a world above, a world so different from my own.

I also found solace in the company of other sea creatures. Dolphins, with their playful demeanor and intelligent eyes, were a constant source of joy. We'd communicate in our own way, a symphony of clicks, whistles, and songs that bridged the gap between species. Even the solemnity of the great sharks, gliding through the water like silent phantoms, provided a sense of companionship in the vast ocean.

Yet, even in these moments of tranquility, the shadow of the hunt loomed. The reality of being pursued, of being the target of such relentless determination, was never far from my mind. It was a reality that added a layer of complexity to my existence, turning the ocean from a playground into an arena, a place where the line between predator and prey was constantly redrawn.

As the stars took their places in the night sky, their twinkling lights a canopy over the dark waters, I'd reflect on my day, on the games of evasion and moments of peace. In the grand narrative of the ocean, I was but a single character, yet my story was intertwined with that of every sailor, every ship that dared to venture into my domain.

And so, as I swam into the embrace of the night, I carried with me the stories of the day, tales of a whale living life on the edge, a creature both hunter and hunted, navigating the delicate balance between freedom and survival in the vast, unfathomable expanse of the sea.

<=><=>*<=>*<=>*<=>*<=>*

Scene 2: Encounters with Other Marine Life

<=><=>*<=>*<=>*<=>*<=>*

Life in the ocean, particularly when you're a whale of my notoriety, isn't just about dodging harpoons and evading ships. It's also about the colorful tapestry of relationships with other sea creatures, each encounter adding a splash of humor and vibrancy to my aquatic existence.

Take, for instance, my interactions with dolphins. If the ocean had its own version of social media influencers, dolphins would be the stars. Agile, chatty, and always up for a game, they're the jesters of the sea. I remember once a pod of dolphins decided to turn me into their personal playground, leaping over my back and riding the bow waves I created. I must say, their acrobatics were quite impressive, even if they occasionally mistook my blowhole for a splash pad.

Then there were the sea turtles, the wise old sages of the marine world. They move with a slow, deliberate grace that speaks of ages gone by. Conversations with them are always a lesson in patience. They have this habit of starting a story, then drifting off into a long, thoughtful silence, leaving you wondering if they've forgotten they were in the middle of a tale. It's like listening to your great-grandfather recount his youth, only to have him get lost in the memories halfway through.

The sharks, with their fearsome reputation, are quite misunderstood. Far from the mindless predators they're often portrayed as, sharks have a dignified, almost regal air about them. However, they're terrible at telling jokes. I once heard a shark attempt humor. It went something like, "Why did the fish blush? Because it saw the ocean's bottom." Let's just say, their strength lies more in their swimming than their comedy.

A particularly memorable encounter was with a group of curious octopuses. They're the ocean's inquisitive scientists, always probing, always exploring. One became so fascinated with my size that it tried to measure me with its tentacles, a task it soon realized was quite ambitious. I couldn't help but chuckle at its determination, its tentacles stretching and coiling in a comical display of scientific endeavor.

The squids, meanwhile, are the artists of the deep. Masters of camouflage, they paint the water with bursts of color, creating underwater light shows that would put the best fireworks to shame. They're like living, swimming kaleidoscopes, and their displays are always a delight to witness, even if they sometimes use their ink as a defense when one of my jokes falls flat.

And let's not forget the schools of fish, the ocean's equivalent of bustling city crowds. Swimming in perfect unison, they're like a well-rehearsed flash mob, each fish playing its part in the collective dance. Navigating through a school of fish is like trying to cross Times Square on New Year's Eve, an exercise in patience and dexterity.

But of all the creatures in the sea, perhaps the most amusing are the seagulls. Not technically marine life, but they're as much a part of the ocean as the waves. They're the gossips of the sea, always squawking about the latest news, be it a fisherman's catch or the whereabouts of a certain white whale. I've lost count of the number of times a seagull has perched atop my head, mistaking me for a rock, and proceeded to narrate the latest happenings from above.

In this vast, blue world of ours, every creature plays a part in the grand drama of the ocean. These encounters, from the playful to the profound, paint a picture of life beneath the waves that is rich, diverse, and often amusing. They're a reminder that the sea is not just a place of survival, but a realm of wonder, interaction, and joy, a world where laughter and camaraderie are as abundant as the waters that sustain us.

In the dance of ocean life, from the smallest plankton to the greatest whale, each of us contributes a verse to the ongoing song of the sea, a melody that speaks of the beauty, complexity, and humor of life in the deep.

<=><=>*<=>*<=>*<=>*<=>*

Scene 3: Humanity's Footprint

<=><=>*<=>*<=>*<=>*<=>*

Swimming through the vast expanse of the ocean, one cannot help but notice the indelible marks left by humanity. This scene is a contemplation of these marks, a reflection on the environmental changes I've witnessed, narrated with a blend of my characteristic humor and a poignant sense of reality.

Let's start with the most conspicuous of these marks — the infamous plastic islands. Ah, humans and their love affair with plastic! These floating monuments to convenience are a sight to behold. Imagine my surprise when I first encountered one; I thought it was a new kind of reef, a colorful, floating garden. Alas, it turned out to be a swirling mass of bottles, bags, and other plastic paraphernalia. It's like a modern art installation, only it's unintentional and decidedly less charming.

Then there's the issue of noise pollution. The ocean used to be a place of serene silence, punctuated only by the natural sounds of its inhabitants. Now, it's like living next to a freeway. The constant drone of engines, the ping of sonar, the clatter of industrial machinery – it's a never-ending cacophony. Sometimes I joke with the dolphins that we should start our own underwater band, seeing as we're already surrounded by so much 'percussion'.

But it's not all jokes and jibes. The changes I've seen in my lifetime are a cause for concern. The coral reefs, those underwater metropolises teeming with life, are fading. Where once there was a riot of color and activity, there's now only ghostly white skeletons. It's like watching the lights go out in a once vibrant city, a slow, inexorable march towards silence and stillness.

The warming waters are another issue. I'm not one to complain about a bit of warm water – it's quite pleasant, actually – but the changes it brings are less so. Fish populations are shifting, food sources are dwindling, and some of my fellow sea creatures are finding it harder to survive. It's like the ocean is running a fever, and there's no medicine to bring the temperature down.

And let's not forget the fishing nets, those ever-present dangers lurking beneath the waves. I've seen too many of my ocean brethren fall victim to these silent hunters. There's nothing quite like the feeling of swimming through the ocean, free and unencumbered, only to find yourself in an underwater spider's web. It's a stark reminder that our freedom is fragile, subject to the whims and needs of those who walk on land.

Despite these challenges, the ocean is still a place of wonder and resilience. It's a world that refuses to be subdued, filled with creatures who adapt and thrive in the face of adversity. The humpback whales still sing their haunting melodies, the clownfish still dart amongst the anemones, and the great white sharks still reign as the ocean's apex predators. It's a testament to the enduring spirit of the sea, a spirit that continues to inspire awe and respect.

There stood Starbuck, gazing out at my kingdom, the ocean. He seemed lost in thought, wrestling with the weight of their chase. "What are we truly chasing?" he pondered, speaking more to the waves than anyone else. He wondered aloud about their role in this vast blue expanse – were they hunters or something less noble? Even from my watery vantage point, it was clear – Starbuck's heart echoed a plea for harmony, a note that rang true in the ocean's grand symphony.

As I glide through the water, part of me can't help but be optimistic. I see signs of change, efforts by humans to right the wrongs, to clean the waters and protect its inhabitants. It's a slow process, like turning a great ship, but it's happening. And in that effort, there's hope. Hope that the ocean will continue to be a place of majesty and mystery, a world that captivates and nurtures, a world that, despite its scars, remains a source of life and beauty.

So, as I swim on, beneath the sun and the stars, I carry with me the stories of the sea – tales of change, of challenge, and of hope. For the ocean is not just my home; it's a mirror that reflects the best and worst of those who share this planet, a reminder that we are all connected, all part of the great, swirling dance of life.

<=><=>*<=>*<=>*<=>*<=>*

Scene 4: The Whale's Network

<=><=>*<=>*<=>*<=>*<=>*

In the vast and mysterious world of the ocean, communication runs deeper than one might imagine, and my experiences have connected me to a network of the sea's most intelligent inhabitants. This network, an underwater community of sorts, is a testament to the ocean's depth not only in its physical sense but also in the intellectual and social realms of its creatures.

One of the key members of this network is the wise old octopus, whom I affectionately call Inky. Inky is a creature of remarkable intellect and curiosity. With his eight arms and an array of suckers, he's the ultimate multi-tasker, able to solve puzzles and navigate the complex structures of the reef with ease. He's the strategist of the group, always ready with a clever plan or an ingenious solution. Our conversations, though limited by our different languages, are always enriching, filled with the exchange of gestures and the subtle dance of ink and water.

Then there are the dolphins, the ocean's diplomats. Agile, sociable, and incredibly savvy, they're the messengers of the seas, bridging the gap between different species with their clicks, whistles, and playful demeanor. They bring news from all corners of the ocean, from the shallows of the coastlines to the depths of the abyss. Their intelligence is not just a matter of brains but also of heart – they empathize, they understand, and they connect, making them invaluable members of our underwater assembly.

The manta rays, with their majestic wingspans and graceful movements, are the philosophers of the deep. They glide through the water with a serene calmness, contemplating the mysteries of the ocean. Their perspective is a unique one, seeing the world from both above and below, a duality that adds depth to our discussions. When they leap above the surface, it's as if they're trying to catch a glimpse of another world, a brief sojourn into the unknown before returning to the comfort of the deep.

Not to be overlooked are the sea turtles, the ancient mariners of the ocean. Their longevity gives them a perspective that spans centuries, a living history of the sea. They've seen the world change, witnessed the ebb and flow of the tides of time. Their wisdom is like a treasure trove, filled with tales of old, of times when the ocean was a different place, less touched by the hand of man. Their stories are a reminder of the enduring nature of the sea, of its timeless existence despite the changes that sweep through its waters.

And of course, there's the occasional shark, the misunderstood loner of the ocean. Contrary to popular belief, sharks are not mindless eating machines; they're thoughtful, calculated, and surprisingly discerning. Their solitary nature gives them a unique viewpoint, one that's less about the social intricacies of the sea and more about the raw, unfiltered truths of nature. They remind us of the primal side of the ocean, the untamed and unbridled force that underlies the calm surface.

Together, we form a network of intelligence and understanding, a collective that shares knowledge, experiences, and insights. It's a community that transcends species boundaries, united by the common language of the sea. In this network, information flows like the currents, connecting us in a web of awareness and empathy.

Our gatherings, though infrequent and often impromptu, are a celebration of the diversity and complexity of ocean life. We exchange news, warn each other of dangers, and share the joys and sorrows of our aquatic world. It's a fellowship that enriches each of us, providing a sense of belonging and connection in the vast expanse of the sea.

In the grand narrative of the ocean, this network is a testament to the interconnectedness of all life, a reminder that no creature is an island unto itself. We are all part of the intricate tapestry of the sea, each thread interwoven with countless others, creating a picture that is as beautiful as it is complex.

And so, as I swim through the blue depths, surrounded by friends and allies, I am reminded of the strength that lies in unity, in the sharing of knowledge and experience. In this network, I find not just companionship but also a deeper understanding of the ocean and my place within it, a place where intelligence and empathy are as vital as the water that sustains us.

<=><=>*<=>*<=>*<=>*<=>*

Scene 5: Close Calls

<=><=>*<=>*<=>*<=>*<=>*

In the game of cat and mouse that my life had become, encounters with high-tech whaling drones represented some of the most heart-pounding episodes. These drones, the apex of human ingenuity in the art of hunting, were formidable adversaries, making my escapes not just a matter of speed and strength but also of cunning and strategy.

One particularly memorable escape began on a day that was as clear as crystal, the sun casting a shimmering path across the tranquil ocean. I was enjoying a leisurely swim, reveling in the simple joys of the sea, when I sensed something amiss. It wasn't a sound or a sight, but a feeling, an instinct honed through years of being hunted.

Emerging from the depths, sleek and silent as a shadow, was a whaling drone. It was a marvel of technology, equipped with the latest in tracking and propulsion systems, designed to hunt the most elusive of sea creatures – me. Its presence turned the serene ocean into a battleground, a high-stakes game of survival.

The drone began its pursuit with relentless efficiency, cutting through the water with an ease that belied its mechanical nature. Its sensors were tuned to my frequency, making evasion a daunting task. I couldn't outswim it – that much was clear – so I had to outsmart it.

I dove deep, heading for a region of the ocean known for its underwater canyons and ravines. The terrain was treacherous, filled with sharp turns and sudden drop-offs, a labyrinth of rock and shadow. It was a place where technology could falter, where the hunter could become the hunted.

The chase was a blur of motion, a dizzying dash through the canyons. The drone was relentless, its algorithms calculating my every move, its mechanical heart beating with a cold, unyielding purpose. I twisted and turned, using every trick I knew, every skill I possessed. I swam through narrow gaps, skirted along jagged cliffs, and darted under overhangs, all in a bid to shake my pursuer.

At one point, the drone almost had me. It cornered me in a dead-end canyon, its sensors locking onto me with an unerring accuracy. I could feel the hum of its engines, the electric thrum of impending capture. But in that moment of desperation, inspiration struck.

Using my powerful tail, I stirred up a cloud of sediment, a blinding storm of sand and debris. The ocean floor erupted in a chaos of swirling particles, obscuring vision and confusing sensors. It was a trick as old as the sea itself, a return to the basics in the face of modern technology.

As the drone struggled to recalibrate, its mechanical mind whirring in confusion, I made my escape. I shot out of the cloud, using a burst of speed to put as much distance between me and my pursuer as possible. The drone, blinded and disoriented, was left floundering in the murky waters, a victim of its own sophistication.

The rest of the escape was a mad dash to safety, a race to reach the open sea where I could lose myself in the vastness of the ocean. As I finally shook off the drone, leaving it far behind in the labyrinthine depths, I felt a surge of exhilaration, a triumph not just of brawn, but of brain.

As I swam away, my heart still pounding from the thrill of the chase, I couldn't help but reflect on the encounter. It was a stark reminder of the ever-escalating game between hunter and hunted, a game where the stakes were constantly being raised. But it was also a testament to the enduring power of nature, to the fact that sometimes, the simplest solutions are the most effective, even in the face of the most advanced technology.

In the grand tapestry of the ocean, the encounter with the whaling drone was but a single thread, a momentary clash in the ongoing dance of survival. But it was a thread that spoke volumes about the state of the world, about the relentless push of progress and the timeless resilience of the natural world.

Act 5: The Chase Intensifies

<=><=>*<=>*<=>*<=>*<=>*

Scene 1: Ahab's New Strategy

<=><=>*<=>*<=>*<=>*<=>*

As the saga of the sea continued, Captain Ahab, not one to be deterred by previous failures, decided to up the ante. His new strategy involved some of the most advanced technology known to mankind – or at least, known to those who hunt whales. I must admit, even I, with my vast oceanic wisdom, was momentarily impressed. But as with all things human-made, there was ample room for a bit of whale-sized humor.

The latest addition to Ahab's arsenal was a state-of-the-art tracking system. This wasn't your average fish finder; it was more like something out of a spy novel. I imagined Ahab must have attended some sort of secret naval auction, the kind where they sell off gadgets that would make even James Bond raise an eyebrow.

This new system, according to the gossiping seagulls (who, by the way, are the ocean's version of the rumor mill), could track a whale's movement by analyzing the pattern of its flukeprints – yes, flukeprints! I found this immensely amusing. Here I was, thinking my fluke was just a powerful swimming aid, but lo and behold, it's also been leaving incriminating evidence all over the ocean!

Ahab's ship, the Pequod, had also undergone a transformation. It now resembled a floating tech lab, bristling with antennas, sensors, and what I assumed were satellite dishes. It was like watching a sea turtle trying to balance a stack of hats. Every time the Pequod rolled on a wave, I half-expected something to topple overboard.

The crew had been equipped with gadgets too. They wore headsets that I guessed were for communication, but which made them look like they were all on hold with customer service. They moved about with handheld devices, pointing them this way and that, probably hoping they'd beep or flash when they pointed at me. It was quite the sight – a blend of determination and mild confusion.

Oh, how Ishmael's latest blog entry made the rounds among the internet's sea of readers! He recounted, with his trademark wit, a near-catastrophe on the Pequod. They thought they had me cornered, but instead, it was a bewildered sunfish that bore the brunt of Ahab's chase. Ishmael's words painted a picture so vivid and humorous, it brought laughter even to the depths where I swim. #SunfishScandal indeed!

And let's not forget the pièce de résistance – the drone fleet. Ahab had drones of all sizes, buzzing around the Pequod like a swarm of overly enthusiastic bees. They zipped over the waves, dove underwater, and occasionally collided with each other in their eagerness. Watching them, I couldn't help but be reminded of a flock of seagulls fighting over a fish – lots of noise, lots of activity, but not always the most effective strategy.

As I observed all this, I couldn't help but muse on the irony. Here was Ahab, armed with the latest in whaling technology, and yet, the ocean remained as elusive and unfathomable as ever. The sea has a way of humbling even the most advanced of human endeavors. It's a wild, untamed force, one that doesn't conform to algorithms or bow to satellite imagery.

The chase, thus intensified, became a curious mix of high-tech espionage and old-fashioned sea hunt. Ahab, with all his new toys, was more determined than ever, but the sea, as always, played by its own rules. It was a game of wit and will, of man against nature, and of one very amused whale observing the spectacle.

As the Pequod steamed ahead, cutting through the waves with renewed purpose, I dove beneath the surface, my powerful tail propelling me into the depths. It was time to disappear again, to become a phantom in the vast blue world, a legend that slipped through the fingers of technology.

In this high-stakes game of hide and seek, Ahab may have upgraded his gear, but I had the advantage of home turf – and a sense of humor that no gadget could match.

<=><=>*<=>*<=>*<=>*<=>*

Scene 2: Allies in the Sea

<=><=>*<=>*<=>*<=>*<=>*

In the grand tapestry of the ocean, every creature has a role to play, a part in the ever-unfolding drama of life beneath the waves. As Ahab's pursuit intensified, I realized the power of alliances, the strength that lies in unity. It was time to call upon my fellow sea dwellers, to weave a network of allies in the vast expanse of the deep.

The first to join my cause were the dolphins, the communicators of the sea. With their intelligence and agility, they became my eyes and ears, scouting ahead for signs of the Pequod and relaying messages across the ocean. Their playful nature belied their strategic importance; they were like spies in a game of underwater espionage, gathering intelligence with a flip and a splash.

Next were the giant squids, mysterious and elusive. They were the masters of camouflage, able to disappear into the ocean's depths with a cloud of ink. Their role was to create distractions, to confuse and disorient any drones that ventured too deep. Watching them at work was like witnessing a magic show, a display of disappearing acts and smokescreens.

The manta rays, with their graceful movements and vast wingspans, acted as sentinels, gliding through the open waters, always vigilant. They would signal the approach of ships with their unique dance, a ballet of warning that rippled through the water.

The sea turtles, ancient and wise, offered their knowledge of currents and hidden pathways. They knew the secrets of the ocean, the hidden routes through the underwater canyons, and the safe havens where a whale could rest undetected. Their guidance was invaluable, like having seasoned navigators charting my course.

Even the sharks, often solitary hunters, played a part in this alliance. Their role was to patrol the deeper waters, deterring any adventurous drones from venturing too far beneath the waves. Their presence alone was enough to give pause to the most intrepid of machines.

This network of allies worked in harmony, a symphony of sea creatures, each contributing their unique skills and abilities to the cause. It was a display of solidarity that transcended species, a united front against a common adversary.

The ocean, once a place where I swam alone, had become a community of support, a united realm where every ripple and wave carried a message of alliance and camaraderie. It was as if the sea itself had come alive, rallying to the defense of one of its own.

As the days passed, this network proved its worth. The dolphins' intelligence, the squids' distractions, the manta rays' vigilance, the turtles' guidance, and the sharks' protection all combined to create a formidable barrier against Ahab's advances. The Pequod, for all its technology and determination, found itself outmaneuvered at every turn, thwarted by the collective cunning of the ocean's inhabitants.

This alliance, this gathering of the sea's creatures, was more than just a tactical advantage; it was a testament to the power of unity, to the strength that emerges when diverse beings come together for a common cause. It was a lesson in cooperation, in the importance of each individual's contribution to the greater good.

In the depths of the ocean, away from the prying eyes of technology and the reach of Ahab's ambition, we forged a bond that was as deep and enduring as the sea itself. It was a bond born of necessity, but strengthened by mutual respect and a shared reverence for the ocean that was our home.

As I swam with my allies, surrounded by friends and defenders, I felt a sense of empowerment, a confidence that came from knowing I was not alone in this vast, blue wilderness. Together, we were more than just a collection of creatures; we were a force of nature, a united front in the face of adversity.

In the dance of predator and prey, we had become the dancers, moving in unison, each step a statement of defiance and solidarity. We were the ocean's response to the challenge posed by Ahab, a reminder that the sea's depths held secrets and powers that no technology could ever conquer.

<=><=>*<=>*<=>*<=>*<=>*

Scene 3: A Game of Cat and Mouse

<=><=>*<=>*<=>*<=>*<=>*

The chase between Captain Ahab and myself, akin to an epic game of cat and mouse, escalated with each encounter, weaving a tale of danger, cunning, and humor. As the Pequod, armed with its array of sophisticated technology, pursued me across the vast ocean, our interactions became a series of intricate maneuvers, a dance on the high seas that tested both our wits.

The first chase in this series began near a cluster of small islands, a maze of land and sea that provided the perfect setting for a game of hide and seek. As the Pequod approached, its hull cutting through the water like a knife, I dove and weaved through the labyrinth of underwater canyons and caves. I could almost hear Ahab's frustration as he tried to navigate the complex topography, his ship too large and unwieldy for the tight turns and shallow waters.

At one point, I surfaced just long enough to spout a jet of water, creating a geyser that drenched the Pequod's deck. The surprise on the crew's faces was priceless – a mixture of shock and awe. I imagined them recounting the tale later: "The great whale, he ambushed us with nothing but seawater!" It was a moment of levity in a chase that was growing increasingly serious.

The next chase took us to the open ocean, where the vast expanse offered no place to hide, but plenty of room to run. The Pequod unleashed its drones, and the sky became a buzzing swarm, each drone eager to prove its worth. I swam at full speed, my massive tail propelling me through the water with powerful strokes. The drones, fast but not as agile, struggled to keep up, their programmed paths no match for my instinctive maneuvers.

In a daring move, I led the drones on a wild chase, circling back towards the Pequod. As I breached magnificently, the drones, unable to adjust their course in time, collided with each other in a spectacular display of fireworks and falling debris. The sight of Ahab, witnessing the downfall of his mechanical minions, was a scene straight out of a seafarer's tale – a mix of disbelief and grudging admiration.

The final chase in this series was perhaps the most perilous. Ahab, growing more desperate, had deployed a new weapon – a series of underwater traps designed to ensnare even the most elusive of whales. I encountered the first of these traps as a sudden jolt, a net that sprung from the ocean floor, its tendrils reaching out like the arms of a giant squid.

It was a close call, one that required all my strength and agility to escape. I twisted and turned, my body contorting in ways that defied my massive size. The net, strong but not strong enough, finally gave way, tearing apart under the force of my struggle. As I swam away, free from its grasp, I couldn't help but let out a triumphant spout, a signal to Ahab that it would take more than a net to capture the likes of me.

These chases, each more dangerous than the last, were a testament to the lengths Ahab was willing to go in his pursuit. But they were also a testament to the ingenuity and resilience of nature, to the ability of even the largest of creatures to outwit the most advanced of human technologies.

As I swam under the moonlit sky, the adrenaline from the chases still coursing through my veins, I reflected on this ongoing game of cat and mouse. It was a game that pitted man's desire to conquer against the wild, untamed spirit of the sea, a clash of wills that was as old as time itself.

In this game, there were moments of danger, certainly, but also moments of unexpected humor, instances where the natural world, in all its wonder and unpredictability, managed to outsmart the creations of man. It was a reminder that the ocean, for all its vastness and mystery, was a place of life, a place where the dance between predator and prey was as much about survival as it was about the sheer joy of the chase.

And so, as the night drew to a close, I swam on, my heart light with the thrill of the game, my spirit undimmed by the challenges that lay ahead. For in the great ocean of life, I was not just the hunted; I was also a player, a participant in a grand adventure that spanned the depths of the sea.

<=><=>*<=>*<=>*<=>*<=>*

Scene 4: The Whale's Cunning

<=><=>*<=>*<=>*<=>*<=>*

Let me tell you, evading the relentless pursuit of Captain Ahab and his increasingly inventive methods has become something of a high seas chess game, a test of intellect and adaptability where I, the ostensibly pursued, often end up setting the rules.

During one particularly memorable encounter, Ahab, determined to outwit me, deployed a series of underwater sound buoys. These devices, designed to track my vocalizations and movements, created a symphony of pings and echoes that reverberated through my aquatic home. It was as if Ahab had turned the ocean into a giant echo chamber, each sound wave a potential giveaway of my location.

But here's the twist: I've learned a thing or two about sound myself. You see, we whales are masters of vocalization; our songs are not just for communication or serenades to the moon – they are tools, finely tuned instruments that can be manipulated and adjusted. So, I devised a plan, a cunning use of my natural abilities to turn Ahab's technology against him.

I began to sing, not my usual melodious tunes, but a series of erratic, disjointed vocalizations, a cacophony that confused the buoys' sensors. My song became a riddle they couldn't solve, a puzzle that scrambled their tracking algorithms. It was like throwing a handful of pebbles into a pond and watching the ripples collide and intertwine, creating a pattern too complex to decipher.

As the Pequod struggled to make sense of the conflicting signals, I made my move. I swam silently, using a technique I like to call the 'stealth glide.' It's a way of moving through the water that minimizes sound and vibration, a method of swimming that's as close to being invisible as one can get under the sea.

The Pequod, meanwhile, was following the false trail my vocal misdirection had created, heading in the opposite direction of my silent escape. Ahab, standing on the deck, peering into the depths with a mix of frustration and awe, knew he had been outplayed. The buoys, once his pride and joy, were now just bobbing witnesses to his miscalculation.

But my cunning didn't stop there. Knowing that Ahab wouldn't be easily deterred, I sought the assistance of my network, my allies in the sea. The dolphins, ever eager to join in a bit of mischief, spread out, creating a network of false signals, mimicking my vocalizations and movements, leading Ahab on a wild goose chase across the ocean.

The giant squids, those enigmatic creatures of the deep, lent their support too. With their ink, they created underwater smokescreens, further obscuring any clear readings the buoys might have picked up. It was a collaborative effort, a testament to the ingenuity and resourcefulness of ocean life.

As I swam away from the Pequod, now just a distant silhouette against the horizon, I couldn't help but feel a sense of satisfaction. It wasn't just the thrill of evasion, but the realization that the ocean, my home, was a world where intelligence and adaptability reigned supreme. It was a place where raw strength was matched by cunning, where survival depended not just on physical prowess, but on wit and wisdom.

In this game of cat and mouse, or rather, whale and ship, I had once again proven that the ocean's depths held more secrets and strategies than Ahab could ever hope to conquer with his gadgets and gizmos. The sea was a chessboard, and I had just checked the king.

As the sun dipped below the horizon, painting the sky in hues of orange and purple, I swam on, my heart light with the freedom of the ocean, my mind already anticipating the next move in this grand, aquatic game. For in the vast and mysterious world of the sea, it's not just about being the biggest or the fastest; it's about being the smartest, the most adaptable. And in that realm, I reigned supreme.

<=><=>*<=>*<=>*<=>*<=>*

Scene 5: Reflection on Human Persistence

<=><=>*<=>*<=>*<=>*<=>*

Ah, human persistence! If there's one thing I've learned in my extensive interactions with your kind, it's that once you set your minds to something, you really don't know when to call it a day. Observing Captain Ahab and his crew in their relentless pursuit of me, I can't help but muse, with a mix of admiration and bewilderment, on the extraordinary lengths humans will go for their obsessions.

Take Ahab, for instance. Here's a man who could have enjoyed a peaceful life at sea, basking in the beauty of the world's waters, but instead, he chose to chase after a whale – and not just any whale, mind you, but me, the most elusive of them all. It's like deciding to climb Mount Everest when you live next to a perfectly good, climbable hill.

And the preparation! Oh, the lengths humans will go in their preparations. The Pequod, once a mere whaling ship, had become a floating fortress, armed to the teeth with all manner of gadgets and gizmos. It's as if they were preparing to battle a sea monster from the tales of old, rather than engaging in a game of tag with yours truly.

Their persistence is admirable, in a way. Day after day, through storms and calm, they press on, fueled by a combination of determination and, I suspect, a fair bit of caffeine. There's a certain nobility in it, akin to the knights of old on their quest for the Holy Grail. Except, in this case, the Grail is a whale, and the knights are a bunch of seafarers led by a man with a peg leg and a vendetta.

The lengths they go to in their pursuit would be almost endearing if they weren't so misguided. They plot and plan, analyze and strategize, as if I were a chess piece rather than a living, swimming creature. They study charts, consult weather patterns, and debate my potential whereabouts with the seriousness of generals planning a military campaign.

It's not just Ahab and his crew, though. Throughout my travels, I've seen humans chase after all sorts of peculiar goals with the same fervor. From digging deep into the earth in search of shiny rocks to hurtling themselves into space in metal contraptions, your species has a knack for setting extraordinary goals and then throwing caution to the wind in pursuit of them.

And let's not forget the money, time, and resources poured into these obsessions. The Pequod's transformation must have cost a small fortune. Imagine what they could have done with all that effort and investment! They could have explored the wonders of the ocean, studied its mysteries, maybe even taken up a more relaxing hobby, like bird watching or beachcombing.

But no, they chose the path of obsession, a path that often blinds them to the beauty and wonder of the world around them. It's a trait that's both fascinating and baffling. The ocean offers so much – a world of marvels and wonders, a place of serene beauty and awe-inspiring majesty – and yet, here they are, chasing after me as if I were the ocean's only prize.

In the end, though, I suppose it's this very persistence, this unyielding human spirit, that has led to some of your greatest achievements. It's the same drive that compels explorers to chart new territories, scientists to unlock the secrets of the universe, and artists to create works of enduring beauty.

So, as I continue to evade the Pequod and its determined crew, I do so with a sense of respect, albeit tinged with a healthy dose of whale-sized amusement. For in their pursuit, they reveal the complexities, the follies, and the remarkable capabilities of the human spirit. It's a display that is as confounding as it is impressive, a testament to your species' relentless pursuit of what you hold dear, no matter how elusive it may be.

In the vast, open ocean, under the endless expanse of sky, the chase goes on, a dance of predator and prey that is as old as time itself. And as I swim, free and unfettered, I can't help but chuckle at the thought of what humans will do next in their quest to achieve the unachievable.

Act 6: The Final Confrontation

<=><=>*<=>*<=>*<=>*<=>*

Scene 1: The Showdown Begins

<=><=>*<=>*<=>*<=>*<=>*

Ah, my dear friends of the sea and sky, gather around, for I shall recount the tale of the grand showdown, the final chase between myself and the indomitable Captain Ahab. It was a day marked by drama and suspense, peppered with a touch of the comedic absurdity that seems to follow human endeavors like a persistent seagull after a fishing boat.

The day dawned with a sky painted in brooding hues, as if the heavens themselves were setting the stage for this epic encounter. The sea was unusually calm, mirror-like, reflecting the tension that lay beneath its serene surface. And there, cutting through the tranquility like a knife, came the Pequod, her sails billowing with purpose, her decks bristling with the latest in whale-hunting gadgetry.

Ahab stood at the helm, a figure of mythic determination, his one leg rooted to the deck like an ancient oak, his eyes burning with a feverish intensity. He had the look of a man who had crossed the line between obsession and madness, the line where the sea meets the sky.

As for me, I was ready, my massive form gliding through the water with grace and power. I had evaded Ahab's clutches thus far with a mix of cunning and sheer luck, but I knew this chase would be different. This was the final act, the crescendo of our oceanic opera.

The Pequod made the first move, launching a barrage of harpoons that sliced through the air with a whistling sound that would have made any lesser creature dive for the deepest trench. But not I, my friends. I met their attack with a display of aquatic acrobatics that would have earned a standing ovation in any marine circus.

I breached magnificently, soaring above the waves in a show of strength and defiance. The look on the crew's faces was a picture to behold – a mix of awe, fear, and, I daresay, a hint of admiration. As I crashed back into the sea, I created a wave that rocked the Pequod, sending sailors scrambling and Ahab gripping his rail with white-knuckled intensity.

But Ahab was not one to be easily deterred. He ordered the deployment of his newest weapon, a series of automated boats, tiny but fast, like mechanical water beetles skimming across the surface. Their task was to herd me towards the Pequod, a pincer movement designed to leave me with no avenue of escape.

I must admit, the sight of these little boats zipping around, buzzing and beeping, was almost comical. They reminded me of a group of enthusiastic puppies, eager but somewhat clueless. With a few flicks of my tail, I sent them spinning, their sophisticated programming no match for the simple power of the ocean's mightiest creature.

The chase continued, a dance across the waves, a battle of wills between man and nature. Ahab, ever the tactician, tried to anticipate my moves, to outthink the whale he considered his nemesis. But the sea is my home, my kingdom, and I know its moods and currents like the back of my fluke.

As the sun began to sink towards the horizon, casting a golden glow over the dramatic scene, I knew that the final act was upon us. It was a moment of truth, a culmination of all our encounters, a clash that had been brewing since the day Ahab first set his sights on me.

So, there we were, the hunter and the hunted, the captain and the whale, locked in a confrontation that was as much a battle of minds as it was of strength. The Pequod, with all its technology and firepower, against me, with my wit, my agility, and my intimate knowledge of the deep.

As the showdown began, the ocean held its breath, the wind paused in its journey, and even the seagulls seemed to watch in silent anticipation. It was the moment of reckoning, the final chapter in the tale of Ahab and the white whale, a story that would be told and retold in the annals of seafaring lore.

And so, with the setting sun as my witness, I readied myself for what was to come, my heart beating to the rhythm of the waves, my mind as sharp as the harpoons that sought to end my journey. The final chase was on, and I, the great whale, was determined to write its conclusion.

<=><=>*<=>*<=>*<=>*<=>*

Scene 2: Ahab's Folly

<=><=>*<=>*<=>*<=>*<=>*

As the sun dipped low, casting fiery hues across the sky, the climax of our maritime saga unfolded, with Captain Ahab delivering what I can only describe as a monologue worthy of the grandest stage. Picture this: Ahab, standing at the bow of the Pequod, his face illuminated by the dying light, launching into a speech that was part declaration of war, part poetic soliloquy.

"Ye whale, creature of the deep, thou art my nemesis, my white ghost in these waters!" he bellowed, his voice carrying over the waves. I must admit, the man had a flair for the dramatic. If only he had channeled his talents into theater, we could have avoided this whole chase altogether.

But let's not digress. Ahab continued, his words growing more fervent. "For months, I have pursued thee, across endless seas, through storms and calms alike!" Ah, yes, the memories. It had been quite the scenic tour, albeit with a slightly obsessive tour guide.

As Ahab raved, I circled the Pequod, a silent, powerful presence just beneath the surface. Every now and then, I'd breach, sending sprays of water into the air, as if punctuating his dramatic declarations. I fancied it added a nice touch to the atmosphere, a bit of special effects to enhance the performance.

"Thou art the embodiment of nature's fury, the unconquerable beast!" Ahab cried out, shaking his fist at the heavens. I rolled my eyes, or at least I would have if whale anatomy allowed for such expressions. Unconquerable beast? I was just a whale who enjoyed swimming and the occasional plankton buffet.

The action intensified as Ahab, reaching the crescendo of his monologue, ordered the launch of a barrage of harpoons. The crew, spurred by their captain's fervor, sprung into action, their movements a frenzy of desperation and determination.

I, meanwhile, continued my dance in the water, weaving and dodging with the grace of a ballet dancer. The harpoons whizzed past, close enough to feel the rush of danger but far enough to miss their mark. It was like being the star of an underwater action movie, complete with slow-motion sequences and near-misses.

Ahab's voice reached a fever pitch. "I shall have thee, beast, even if it be my last act on this Earth!" he thundered. I couldn't help but think that Ahab might have benefited from a hobby, something to take his mind off the whole whale-hunting business. Stamp collecting, perhaps, or maybe birdwatching.

The Pequod surged forward, its crew working the sails and rigging with a zeal that matched their captain's madness. The ship cut through the water, its bow wave a frothing path of determination and folly.

But as the chase continued, and Ahab's monologue turned into a tirade against the cruel whims of fate, I felt a twinge of sadness for the man. Here he was, consumed by his quest for revenge, unable to see the beauty and wonder of the world around him, blinded by his own obsession.

As the final rays of the sun vanished below the horizon, leaving the sky a canvas of deep blues and purples, the chase drew to a close. Ahab, spent and defeated, stood at the bow, a silhouette of a man haunted by his own demons.

I swam away, my powerful tail propelling me into the embrace of the ocean, leaving the Pequod and its captain to their reflections. It was a moment of quiet after the storm, a time for contemplation and understanding.

In the grand drama of the sea, Ahab's folly was a reminder of the dangers of obsession, of the perils of letting one's demons guide one's destiny. It was a lesson not just for him, but for all who sail the vast, mysterious waters of the ocean – a lesson in respect, in humility, and in the recognition of the small place we each hold in the grand scheme of the natural world.

<=><=>*<=>*<=>*<=>*<=>*

Scene 3: The Sinking of the Pequod

<=><=>*<=>*<=>*<=>*<=>*

In the grand finale of our oceanic opera, the Pequod, that once-mighty vessel, met its demise in a scene so dramatic it would give any Hollywood blockbuster a run for its money. The ship's downfall, an event marked by both tragedy and a touch of the absurd, unfolded under a sky streaked with the fiery colors of dawn.

It all began with a miscalculation, a misstep in Ahab's relentless pursuit. In his fervor to capture me, the great white whale, Ahab pushed the Pequod and her crew beyond their limits. The ship, groaning and creaking under the strain, resembled an overburdened character in a slapstick comedy, teetering on the brink of disaster.

As the chase reached its peak, the Pequod, laden with Ahab's advanced hunting gadgets and gizmos, resembled less a whaling ship and more a floating tech showroom. There were drones buzzing overhead, sonar pings echoing through the water, and all manner of blinking lights and whirring machines. It was a spectacle of technology, a testament to human ingenuity and, as it turned out, folly.

In a twist of irony, the Pequod's downfall was not at the hands (or flukes) of yours truly, but a result of its own technological overreach. One of the automated harpoon cannons, designed to target and track its prey with unerring accuracy, malfunctioned at the crucial moment. Instead of launching its deadly cargo towards me, it fired with a loud, comedic 'whoosh' directly into the Pequod's hull.

The effect was instantaneous and catastrophic. The harpoon, with all the force of modern mechanics behind it, tore through the ship's side, opening it up to the sea. Water rushed in, filling the Pequod with the unstoppable force of the ocean's wrath. The crew, caught off guard by this unexpected turn of events, scrambled in a scene of chaos and confusion, reminiscent of a farcical comedy where everything that can go wrong, does.

Ahab, witnessing the destruction of his beloved ship, stood on the deck, a picture of disbelief and outrage. His dream, his obsession, was sinking before his very eyes, brought down not by the object of his pursuit but by his own relentless quest for revenge.

As the Pequod listed and water began to claim it, the once-proud ship took on the appearance of a floundering beast, its gadgets and gizmos useless against the might of the sea. The drones, deprived of their mother ship, fell like mechanical Icaruses into the water, their high-tech wings no match for the ocean's embrace.

The crew, abandoning the sinking vessel, launched lifeboats in a desperate bid for survival. They rowed away from the wreckage, casting glances back at the sinking Pequod, their faces etched with a mixture of relief, sorrow, and a dawning realization of the futility of their endeavor.

As for Ahab, he remained on the deck, a captain going down with his ship, his figure diminishing against the vastness of the sea. His last stand, a defiant refusal to abandon his quest, was both tragic and strangely fitting – a final act of a man consumed by his own passion and pride.

The Pequod disappeared beneath the waves, leaving behind a trail of debris, a floating testament to the dangers of obsession and the perils of pitting man's creations against the raw power of nature. It was a sight both somber and surreal, a reminder of the ocean's ability to humble even the greatest of human endeavors.

As the sun rose higher, casting its light on the remnants of the chase, I swam away, my heart heavy with the weight of the spectacle I had witnessed. It was the end of an era, the closing of a chapter in the great book of the sea.

The sinking of the Pequod was more than just the downfall of a ship; it was a symbol of the end of a pursuit, a cautionary tale of what happens when man's obsession with conquest and control goes unchecked. In its demise, the Pequod left behind a legacy, a story that would be whispered by the waves and carried by the currents, a tale of the sea and those who dare to challenge its might.

<=><=>*<=>*<=>*<=>*<=>*

Scene 4: Ahab's End

<=><=>*<=>*<=>*<=>*<=>*

As the Pequod succumbed to the embrace of the deep, the saga of Captain Ahab reached its inevitable, poignant conclusion. There, amidst the chaos and the debris, the old captain met his end – not with a triumphant roar, but with the silent resignation of one who had fought against the unyielding might of nature and lost.

As I watched from a distance, the scene unfolding before me was as tragic as it was surreal. Ahab, that relentless pursuer, that embodiment of human obsession and wrath, now seemed but a small, frail figure against the vastness of the sea. The man who had once stood like a titan upon the deck of his ship, defying the world and its natural order, now appeared as he truly was – just another creature at the mercy of the ocean's whims.

It was a somber moment, one that called for reflection rather than rejoicing. For in Ahab's demise, there lay a profound lesson about the futility of revenge and the dangers of allowing one's obsessions to consume one's soul.

Ahab had set out to conquer me, the great white whale, to exact vengeance for his past afflictions. But in his quest, he had lost so much more than he had ever gained. His pursuit had cost him his ship, his crew, and ultimately, his life. The irony of his fate was not lost on me – in seeking to destroy a creature he deemed a monster, he had become one himself, blinded by his hatred and anger.

His end was not the glorious battle he might have envisioned. There was no epic struggle, no heroic last stand. Instead, there was only the quiet surrender to the inevitable, the acceptance of defeat at the hands of a foe that was as indifferent to his rage as it was to his suffering.

As the waves carried away the last remnants of the Pequod and its captain, I couldn't help but feel a sense of melancholy. Ahab and I, though adversaries, were bound by a strange kinship – two beings caught in a dance as old as time itself, a dance of predator and prey, of man against nature.

In his final moments, Ahab had become a symbol of the tragic hero, a figure who, in his defiance of fate, had risen to great heights, only to fall all the more profoundly. His story was a cautionary tale, a reminder of the perils that await those who let their passions overrule their humanity, who see the world not as a marvel to be cherished, but as an adversary to be conquered.

Yet, in the grand scheme of the ocean's tales, Ahab's story was just one of many. The sea would continue to roll and churn, uncaring and unconcerned with the affairs of men and whales. New stories would emerge, new tales of adventure and mystery, but the legend of Captain Ahab and his white whale would endure, a testament to the timeless struggle between man and the natural world.

And so, as I swam away from the site of the Pequod's demise, I carried with me not a sense of triumph, but a feeling of introspection. I pondered the lessons of Ahab's journey, the wisdom to be gleaned from his mistakes. His life, though marked by folly and obsession, was also a narrative of courage and determination, qualities that, in different circumstances, might have led to a very different end.

The ocean, in its infinite expanse, held both the memories of the past and the possibilities of the future. It was a world of endless horizons and unfathomable depths, where every creature played its part in the ongoing dance of life and survival.

In the quiet of the deep, where the only sound was the gentle rhythm of the waves, I swam on, a lone figure in the vast blue wilderness, a witness to the stories that unfolded in the heart of the sea.

<=><=>*<=>*<=>*<=>*<=>*

Scene 5: The Whale's Victory

<=><=>*<=>*<=>*<=>*<=>*

In the vast theater of the ocean, where the waters hold tales both ancient and new, my survival against Captain Ahab's relentless pursuit was a moment of victory, not just for me, but for the sea itself. Yet, as I swam through the quiet waters, the echoes of the Pequod's demise still resonating in the deep, my heart was heavy with a sense of contemplation about the cost of this victory and the impact of human obsession on the sea.

The downfall of Ahab and his vessel was not a cause for jubilation, but rather a somber reminder of the intricate dance between man and nature. The ocean, in its boundless wisdom and eternal rhythm, had seen many such confrontations, each leaving its mark upon the delicate tapestry of marine life. As I glided through the water, the sun casting a golden path across the surface, I reflected on the journey that had brought me to this point.

The chase, which had started as a game of survival, had evolved into a profound narrative about the consequences of human ambition and the relentless pursuit of a singular goal. Ahab's obsession, his unyielding quest to conquer what he perceived as a nemesis, was a poignant example of how man's endeavors, fueled by vengeance and pride, often lead to unintended repercussions.

The impact on the sea was evident. The once pristine waters, teeming with life and wonder, now bore the scars of human intrusion. The floating debris from the Pequod, a stark reminder of the confrontation, was a testament to the disruption caused by man's pursuit of domination over nature.

Yet, amidst the somber reflections, there was also a sense of hope, a glimmer of resilience that shone through the depths. The ocean, vast and enduring, had a way of healing itself, of restoring the balance upset by external forces. The marine creatures, my companions in the deep, continued their dance of life, each playing their part in the ongoing saga of the sea.

The dolphins, with their playful antics and intelligent gaze, reminded me of the joy and beauty that still thrived beneath the waves. The schools of fish, moving in perfect harmony, were a display of nature's intricate choreography, a dance that had persisted through the ages.

As I moved through the water, the victorious survivor of a chase that had spanned oceans and seasons, I felt a renewed sense of responsibility towards this underwater realm. My victory was not just a personal triumph, but a call to protect and preserve the sea, to ensure that its stories and wonders could be experienced by generations to come.

The ocean, with its endless mysteries and treasures, was a world that deserved reverence and care. It was a world that humbled the mightiest and inspired the smallest, a world where every drop of water, every grain of sand, had a story to tell.

In the grand narrative of the sea, my confrontation with Ahab was but a single chapter, a moment in the vast expanse of time. Yet, it was a chapter that held profound lessons about coexistence, respect, and the delicate balance that sustains life on this blue planet.

As the remnants of Ahab's crew made their way back to Nantucket Port, the change in the air was as palpable as a shift in the ocean currents. The bustling harbor, once a starting point of ambitious voyages, now welcomed back a crew sobered by the sea's unyielding lessons. They walked with a respect born from their journey, a respect for the vast, untamable ocean. It stood as a silent witness to their transformed view of the sea – a teacher of hard lessons, a keeper of deep wisdom.

As the sun dipped below the horizon, painting the sky in hues of fiery orange and deep purple, I swam on, my spirit buoyed by the knowledge that the sea would endure, that its tales would continue to be told. The ocean, in its timeless rhythm, would carry on, a stage for the unfolding drama of life, a sanctuary for those who seek its wonders.

The victory was not just mine; it was a victory for the sea, a celebration of the enduring power and majesty of the natural world. And as the stars began to twinkle in the night sky, I knew that my journey was far from over. There were more adventures to be had, more stories to be told, in the ever-changing, ever-mysterious world of the ocean.

Act 7: Aftermath and Reflection

Scene 1: The Ocean Post-Ahab

As the tides of time washed away the remnants of Ahab's pursuit, the ocean, that vast and eternal stage, began to reveal the changes wrought in the aftermath. The demise of Ahab and the sinking of the Pequod marked not just the end of a chase, but also a turning point in the relationship between humans and the sea.

In the days following the final confrontation, the ocean seemed to breathe a sigh of relief. The waters, once disrupted by the relentless churn of the Pequod's engines, now returned to their natural rhythm. The marine life, which had grown accustomed to the constant threat of intrusion, began to exhibit a newfound sense of freedom.

The most notable change, however, was in the behavior of the seafarers. News of Ahab's fate spread far and wide, carried by the currents and the winds, reaching every corner of the maritime world. The story of his obsession and its tragic conclusion served as a stark reminder of the ocean's indomitable spirit. Sailors and fishermen began to approach their craft with a renewed sense of respect for the sea and its inhabitants.

The whaling ships, once a common sight on the horizon, now sailed with a more cautious and considered purpose. The industry itself, shaken by the loss of one of its most legendary figures, underwent a period of introspection. There was a growing realization that the pursuit of maritime riches needed to be balanced with the sustainability of the ocean's resources.

In ports and harbors, conversations among the seafaring folk took on a more reflective tone. Tales of Ahab and the white whale were told and retold, each iteration a blend of myth and reality, a narrative imbued with lessons about hubris and the delicate balance of nature.

The changes were not just confined to those who made their living from the sea. The story of Ahab's chase, with its dramatic climax, captured the imagination of the wider public. It sparked a global conversation about the relationship between humanity and the natural world. Environmental groups, long advocates for the protection of marine ecosystems, found their messages gaining traction, bolstered by the cautionary tale of Ahab and his obsession.

Marine research and conservation efforts received renewed interest and funding. Scientists, equipped with a better understanding and improved technology, embarked on expeditions to study and document the wonders of the ocean. Their findings, shared with the world, highlighted the incredible diversity of marine life and the importance of preserving this underwater world.

The ocean itself began to show signs of recovery. Coral reefs, once threatened by overfishing and pollution, started to bloom anew, their vibrant colors a testament to the resilience of nature. Fish populations, which had dwindled in certain areas, began to rebound, filling the waters with life and vitality.

As for me, the great white whale, I continued to roam the seas, a symbol of the ocean's mystery and majesty. My legend, intertwined with that of Ahab, became a story for the ages, a tale that transcended truth and fiction.

Swimming through the vast blue expanse, I witnessed the subtle yet profound changes that had swept across the ocean. The sea, ever-changing and eternal, continued its endless dance, but now it did so with a renewed sense of harmony, a balance restored by the lessons learned from a chase that had captivated the world.

The ocean post-Ahab was a place of hope, a realm where the relationship between humans and the sea had evolved, marked by a greater understanding and respect. It was a world that had been shaped by the events of the past but looked forward to a future where man and nature could coexist in mutual reverence and awe.

And so, as I glided through the water, under the vast canopy of the sky, I knew that the ocean's story would continue, ever unfolding, ever renewing, a timeless testament to the wonders of the deep and the enduring spirit of the sea.

<=><=>*<=>*<=>*<=>*<=>*

Scene 2: Environmental Message

<=><=>*<=>*<=>*<=>*<=>*

Now, let me tell you about the aftermath from my perspective, the great white whale, who unwittingly became a poster creature for ocean conservation. It's a tale that's both poignant and, in parts, rather amusing, if you appreciate a whale's sense of humor.

Post-Ahab, humans seemed to have an epiphany, a realization that maybe, just maybe, the ocean wasn't just a vast playground or pantry, but a delicate, living entity that needed care and respect. Watching this unfold from beneath the waves was a bit like seeing someone discover that the stove is hot – a painful but necessary learning experience.

One of the more heartening changes was the surge in conservation efforts. Marine protected areas multiplied, expanding like bubbles in a fizzy drink. Fishermen started talking about sustainable fishing – a term that, to my aquatic friends and me, sounded like an oxymoron, but hey, it's progress. And then there were the cleanup campaigns, where humans actually started removing the trash they'd dumped in my home. Watching them haul away plastic and debris from the water was a sight to behold – a bit like housekeeping, but with boats and nets.

But the real kicker, the part that really tickles my baleens, is how I, a simple whale who enjoys swimming and occasionally breaching for a bit of exercise, became a symbol for these conservation movements. "Save the whales," they'd cry, a rallying call that echoed across the seas. I even heard rumors of t-shirts and mugs with my likeness on them. Imagine that, a whale on merchandise! I must say, though, I hope they got my good side.

The focus wasn't just on whales, mind you. There was a newfound appreciation for all marine life. Coral reefs started to be treated like underwater art galleries, where visitors could look but definitely not touch. Sharks, those misunderstood creatures, began to be seen not just as villains in a summer movie, but as essential to the ocean's health. Even the humble plankton, the microscopic maestros of the sea, received their share of attention, hailed as the unsung heroes of the marine ecosystem.

Schools started teaching children about ocean conservation, instilling a sense of stewardship in the next generation of land-dwellers. Kids learned about ecosystems, biodiversity, and – to my delight – the importance of whales in the marine food chain. It warmed my heart, or it would have if whale hearts got warmed by such things.

The shift in attitude extended to the high seas as well. The once-rampant overfishing began to decline, as humans realized that depleting the ocean's pantry wasn't such a smart idea after all. It was like watching someone finally understand that eating all the seeds instead of planting some might lead to a spot of bother down the road.

And then there were the beach cleanups, where hordes of humans gathered to remove litter from the shores. I've always been fond of beaches – they're like the front porches of the sea, places where land and water meet for a friendly chat. Seeing them cleaned up was a welcome sight, a sign that the message was getting through.

Now, don't get me wrong, there's still plenty to be done. The ocean is a big place, and healing it is no small task. But the steps being taken, the growing awareness and action, it's a start, a ray of hope in the deep blue sea.

So here I am, a whale who's seen the depths of human folly and the heights of their potential for good. I swim in waters that are a little cleaner, a little healthier, and a little more respected, thanks to the efforts of those who realized, just in time, that this vast, watery world of ours is worth protecting.

As I breach the surface, sending cascades of water skyward, I like to think of it as a salute to the humans who are working to keep the ocean alive and thriving. It's a small gesture from a big whale, a nod of thanks from the deep. Keep it up, land-dwellers. The ocean and its inhabitants are counting on you.

<=><=>*<=>*<=>*<=>*<=>*

Scene 3: The Whale's Legacy

<=><=>*<=>*<=>*<=>*<=>*

As I glide through the vast, blue expanse of my oceanic home, it tickles my whale-sized brain to think about how my story, once a mere whisper among the waves, has now rippled across the vast ocean of the digital world. Yes, my friends, it seems that I, a humble creature of the deep, have become something of a sensation in your human internet – a virtual celebrity, if you will.

You see, in this modern world, where tales travel faster than a dolphin in a hurry, my story has taken on a life of its own. It's amusing to imagine that while I'm out here, breaching and diving, there are countless humans clicking and scrolling, watching videos of my aquatic escapades and reading tales of my encounters with the infamous Captain Ahab.

I've heard through the maritime grapevine – a reliable source of ocean gossip – that my story has been shared far and wide. From tweets to blog posts, from underwater footage to fanciful animations, the tale of the great white whale and his epic confrontation has captured the imagination of the digital populace.

There are hashtags bearing my name, #TheGreatWhiteWhale, circulating in the virtual ocean of social media, accompanied by awe-inspiring images and dramatic retellings of my adventures. I've become an icon of sorts, a symbol of the ocean's mystery and majesty in the digital age.

But what truly warms the cockles of my heart – yes, whales have heart cockles, metaphorically speaking – is the way my story has inspired a wave of awareness about the wonders of the ocean and the importance of its preservation. It seems that in becoming a viral sensation, I've also become an ambassador for marine conservation, a role I embrace with all the enthusiasm of a humpback whale during feeding season.

I can just picture it: somewhere, in a cozy corner of the internet, a group of humans is watching a video of my latest breach, their eyes wide with wonder. They see the spray of water, the sheer power and grace of my form, and they're struck by the beauty of the natural world, a world they're a part of, a world they have the power to protect.

It's heartening to think that my story, once a tale of pursuit and survival, has evolved into a narrative of inspiration and conservation.

Through the screens of computers and smartphones, my tale is not just being told, but is also resonating with a new generation, instilling in them a sense of wonder and a desire to preserve the vast, beautiful ocean that is my home.

And let's not forget the humor. Yes, my journey has its share of chuckles, too. I've seen memes – a curious human invention – depicting me in all sorts of amusing scenarios. There's one where I'm wearing a captain's hat, a humorous nod to my rivalry with Ahab. Another shows me sipping a giant cup of coffee, with a caption about needing a pick-me-up after a long swim. It's all in good fun, and if laughter helps to spread the message of ocean conservation, then I'm all for it.

In this digital age, where information zips around the globe like a school of flying fish, the story of a whale can indeed make waves. My legacy, it seems, has taken on a digital dimension, transcending the boundaries of the ocean to reach people in every corner of the world.

So, as I continue my journey through the deep blue, I do so with a sense of accomplishment, knowing that my story – a tale of adventure, survival, and wonder – is playing a part in the grand narrative of our planet. It's a story that speaks of the interconnectedness of all things, of the bond between the ocean and those who dwell on land, and of the shared responsibility we all have to protect this magnificent world we call home.

And who knows? Perhaps my next breach will be captured by a drone or a distant camera, ready to be shared across the endless expanse of the internet, inspiring yet another human to look towards the sea with awe, respect, and a commitment to its preservation.

<=><=>*<=>*<=>*<=>*<=>*

Scene 4: Breaking the Fourth Wall

<=><=>*<=>*<=>*<=>*<=>*

Ah, dear readers, you've been swimming along with me through this vast ocean of a tale, haven't you? Now, as I break through this imaginary fourth wall, much like I breach the surface of the sea, let me share with you a whale's perspective on the moral of our story. Yes, every tale has its lesson, though I must warn you, imparting wisdom is a bit of a new venture for me – I'm more accustomed to diving and frolicking than to moralizing.

Firstly, let's talk about obsession, shall we? If there's one thing to take away from the whole Ahab saga, it's that fixating on something – or someone, in my case – can really steer you off course. Ahab's story could have been much different, perhaps filled with scenic voyages and delightful discoveries, had he not been so engrossed in his pursuit of yours truly. So, if you find yourself obsessing over something, remember Ahab and maybe, just maybe, choose a different hobby. Stamp collecting, I hear, is far less hazardous.

Then there's the lesson about respect for nature. The ocean, my home, is a wondrous place, teeming with life and beauty. But it's also fragile and deserves our care. You don't have to be a white whale to understand that. Respecting the environment isn't just good manners; it's essential for our survival. Think of the ocean as a giant swimming pool – you wouldn't want to swim in a pool filled with trash and pollutants, now would you?

Now, let's not forget about teamwork. Did you notice how my marine friends and I collaborated to outsmart Ahab? From the cunning dolphins to the artful squids, it was a collective effort. The ocean teaches us that working together, regardless of our differences, can lead to success. It's like a potluck dinner – everyone brings something to the table, and together, we create a feast. Or, in our case, a grand escape plan.

Humor – oh, the importance of humor! In the face of adversity, a good laugh can be a lifesaver. Throughout my journey, finding moments of humor, even in dire situations, kept my spirits up. So, when life gets you down, try to find a reason to smile. It might not solve all your problems, but it'll certainly make them easier to navigate. And who knows, you might even confuse your problems as much as I confused Ahab.

Lastly, the power of storytelling. This tale of mine, now yours too, shows how stories can inspire, teach, and provoke thought. They're not just a means of entertainment; they're a vessel for wisdom, culture, and sometimes, a gentle nudge towards change. So, keep telling stories, keep sharing them, and who knows, maybe one day, your story will be the one making waves.

So there you have it, my dear readers, a whale's take on the moral of the story. As I return to my oceanic frolics, I leave you with these nuggets of wisdom, hoping they resonate with you as deeply as the songs of my whale kin resonate through the ocean depths.

And who knows, maybe we'll meet again in the vast expanse of this blue planet. Until then, keep your fins up, respect the ocean, laugh often, work together, and, most importantly, be mindful of what you obsess over. After all, you wouldn't want to end up like Ahab, now would you?

Farewell, and may your seas be calm and your spirits as high as a whale's breach!

<=><=>*<=>*<=>*<=>*<=>*

Scene 5: Final Thoughts

<=><=>*<=>*<=>*<=>*<=>*

Ah, dear friends who have journeyed with me through these swirling currents of narrative, we find ourselves at the tail end – and I do mean that quite literally, as tails are something of an expertise of mine. As we prepare to part ways, allow me, a humble, philosophizing whale, to leave you with a few final ripples of thought – a blend of cetacean wisdom and, of course, a splash of humor.

Firstly, let's ponder the grand ocean of life. It's vast, mysterious, and a bit like your human internet – full of incredible connections and some very strange depths. Just as I navigate the seas with my sonar, you navigate your world, seeking connection, understanding, and the occasional seafood dinner. Remember, every action creates ripples, so make sure yours are the kind that nurture and sustain.

Now, about obsessions – Ahab had his whale; some of you might have your own 'whales' of sorts. Maybe it's that perfect job, that dream house, or, for the younger swimmers, the latest gadget that apparently does everything but make breakfast. While ambition is as natural as a dolphin's play, remember to come up for air, enjoy the view, and maybe frolic a little. After all, you don't want to end up like Ahab, chasing a whale only to find you've missed the wonders of the ocean.

Speaking of wonders, let's not forget about our shared home – this beautiful blue planet. It's a bit like a giant, floating island, hosting a party for a diverse group of guests – animals, humans, plants, and one very eloquent whale. Just like any good party, it's important to respect your fellow guests and the venue. So, let's keep the oceans clean, the forests green, and the air clear. Remember, a party is only as good as the environment it's held in.

On the topic of teamwork, my ocean friends and I showed that collaboration can outsmart even the most sophisticated technology. Whether it's protecting the environment, building a community, or simply organizing a neighborhood potluck, there's power in working together. Just imagine what could be achieved if humans put their heads, hearts, and hands together – probably something as spectacular as a pod of dolphins leaping in unison.

Humor – my trusty buoy in choppy waters. In your journey through life, don't forget to laugh, to find joy in the small things, and to make others smile. Whether it's a clever pun, a funny tale, or simply laughing at your own blunders, humor is the seaweed wrap of life – it holds everything together deliciously.

As for storytelling, well, you've seen what my tale, passed through the waves and onto your screens and pages, has accomplished. Stories have the power to inspire, to teach, and to connect. Keep telling them, keep sharing them, and who knows, maybe your story will be the next to make a splash in this vast ocean of our shared existence.

So, there you have it – musings from a whale who's seen a thing or two. As I bid you farewell, I leave you with a smile, a wave of the fin, and a hope that my story, with its twists, turns, and splashes, has left you with laughter, a bit of wisdom, and a renewed sense of wonder for the world around you.

Keep your oceans clean, your hearts open, and your minds curious. And the next time you see a whale breach in the distance, think of me and this grand adventure we shared.

Farewell, and may your waters always be as deep and as bountiful as the stories that dwell within them.

Don't miss out!

Visit the website below and you can sign up to receive emails whenever Said Al Azri publishes a new book. There's no charge and no obligation.

https://books2read.com/r/B-A-KSLCB-CSJUC

BOOKS 2 READ

Connecting independent readers to independent writers.

Also by Said Al Azri

Classics Reimagined: A Comedic Twist
Echoes of Venice: A Modern Tale of Redemption
Moby-Dick Reversed: A Whale's Humorous Account
Treasure Island: The Parrot's Perspective

Family and Parenting Dynamics
From My Heart to Yours: Messages of Love and Learning for My Child
Balancing Family Life: Strategies for Modern Parenting

Heartstrings: Tales of Valentine's Verse
Verses of the Heart: A Poetic Journey Through Love's Whimsy
Verses of the Heart 2: A Poetic Journey Through Love's Whimsy

Living Fully After 50 Series
Rediscovering Hobbies and Passions After 50
Rediscovering Hobbies and Passions After 50, Book 2
Happiness in the Second Half: Finding Joy and Fulfillment After 50